"Tomorrow night we'll shoot John Stone."

"What if Chopak already got him?" asked Ramsey.

Casey inhaled his cigarette and blew smoke into the air. "If Chopak already got him, then we can't get him twice. But if Chopak didn't get him, then we'll find him and shoot him down like a dog. Then we'll tie him up behind one of our horses and drag his body through town. We'll show them people what kind of hero he is, and then we'll hit that bank again, only this time we'll take every penny out of it."

He held the cigarette between his fingers, and its tip glowed cherry red in the darkness. "Nobody messes with the Deke Casey gang and gets away with it," he said. "John Stone has got to die."

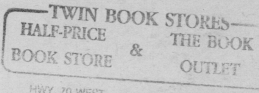

SEARCHER

TIN BADGE

Josh Edwards

DIAMOND BOOKS, NEW YORK

TIN BADGE

A Diamond Book / published by arrangement
with the author

PRINTING HISTORY
Diamond edition / February 1991

ISBN: 1-55773-463-1

Diamond Books are published by
The Berkley Publishing Group,
200 Madison Avenue, New York, New York 10016.
The name "DIAMOND" and its logo
are trademarks belonging to Charter Communications, Inc.

PRINTED IN THE UNITED STATES OF AMERICA

10 9 8 7 6 5 4 3 2 1

TIN BADGE

1

THE CLOCK ON the side of the bank said ten o'clock in the morning as John Stone rode past. His clothes were matted and worn; he wore a growth of beard and was covered with dust and dirt. His big black horse had a wild look in his eyes as he bucked his head up and down and plodded amid carriages and other riders on horseback, his hoofbeats pounding on the ground.

Stone was entering Petie, a large town of freshly painted wooden buildings, many of them two and three stories high. He'd been on the trail eight days without seeing another human being, and in the saddle since sunup. All he wanted to do was get off his horse and take a look at civilization again.

He angled the horse to the curb, climbed to the dirt, and tied the bridle to the hitching rail. Loosening the cinch strap of the saddle, Stone ducked under the rail and climbed onto the planked sidewalk.

It creaked under the weight of numerous pedestrians. Many of the men were nattily dressed in frock coats, shirts, and ties, while the ladies wore the latest fashions from the East, with bonnets on their heads and the hems of their dresses touching the boardwalk. Stone dropped onto an empty bench in front of a pawnshop, beneath the three big brass balls.

He pushed his old Confederate cavalry officer's hat back and reached for his bag of tobacco, his long legs sprawled in front of him. He was six feet two, and his pants were tucked into the bottoms of high-topped black boots, cavalry style. He rolled himself a cigarette with strong rough hands, and wore a black bandanna around his throat. His eyes were blue, his cheeks deeply tanned, and he had dark blond hair. He wore two Colt pistols low and tied down on crisscrossing gunbelts.

It was a warm summer day, and the sun shone brightly in the sky. Stone put the cigarette into his mouth and lit it up. Across the street were a barbershop, hardware store, and the Paradise Saloon. Petie had the look of a prosperous town, civilized and law-abiding, unlike the rowdy little conglomerations of shacks and outhouses that Stone usually had found on the frontier.

Somebody dropped beside him on the bench. Stone turned and saw a bony old man wearing a floppy cowboy hat and carrying a cracked guitar with one string missing. The old man smiled, revealing a toothless mouth. His nose was a mangled red lump in the middle of his lined and wrinkled face.

"I ain't never see'd you before," the old man said. "You must be new around here."

"Just arrived."

"Where you from?"

"South Carolina originally."

"Know somebody in town?"

"No."

"You look like you need a drink."

"I'll get one as soon as I take care of my horse. You been in Petie long?"

"Before you was ever thought of."

Stone reached into his shirt pocket and pulled out a photograph in a silver frame, covered with isinglass. "Ever see this woman?"

The old man took the picture and squinted his rheumy eyes. The photograph showed a pretty young blonde wearing a high-necked gown. She was smiling, gazing to the side of the photographer.

"You're damn right I seen her," the old man declared. "She's Doreen Eckles." He pointed across the street to the Paradise Saloon. "She works right over thar."

Stone stared at him in astonishment. He'd been looking for the woman in the picture ever since the Civil War, roaming the frontier like a vagabond, and she was suddenly across the street?

"Are you sure?" he asked.

"Sure I'm sure. I seen her jest a few minutes ago. C'mon, I'll take you to her."

Stone got up from the bench, towering over the old man. The woman he was looking for was named Marie Higgins, but maybe she'd changed her name.

They crossed the street side by side, Stone walking slowly so the old man wouldn't have to struggle to keep up. The old man was bandy-legged and smelled like tobacco, whiskey, and sweat.

"What's yer name?" the old man asked.

"John Stone."

"I'm Toby Muldoon."

They shook hands. A stagecoach clattered by in front of them, pulled by a team of eight frothing horses. The guard sat on the box beside the driver, his rifle cradled in his hands, the stagecoach's wheels churning up dust. It passed, and Stone looked ahead at the Paradise Saloon. After all these years, could it be that Marie was across the street?

They'd been engaged to wed before the war, and then he'd gone off to fight for Bobby Lee, leaving her behind. Four years later he returned, and she'd disappeared, his parents were dead, and their plantation had been burned to the ground by Sherman's army. Some folks said Marie had gone west with a Union officer, but Stone couldn't believe Marie would've gone anywhere with a Yankee, but he'd come west looking for her anyway. He'd had nothing else to do, nothing better to hope for. Marie was the love of his life and he'd never been able to forget her.

His heart quickened as he approached the boardwalk on the far side of the street. Muldoon pushed the doors open, and Stone followed him into a spacious drinking establishment with the bar straight ahead and round tables scattered across the floor. Although it was morning, a fair-sized crowd was gathered, guzzling whiskey, playing cards, talking loudly. Above the bar was a large painting showing naked women cavorting in a meadow.

"Right this way," said Muldoon, as if he owned the place.

He headed toward the bar, and behind it a young woman with long straight black hair was working. She looked as though she might be part Indian, and was tall, wearing a low-cut blouse with a flower print on it, and a dark brown leather skirt.

Muldoon stopped in front of the bar and grinned, showing his gums and the tip of his leathery tongue. "There she is!" he said proudly.

"Where?"

Muldoon pointed to the woman behind the bar. "Her."

"She doesn't look anything like the woman I showed you in the picture!"

"Shore she does."

The woman behind the bar was drawing a mug of beer from a brass spigot. "That old fart botherin' you, mister? He'll do anything for a drink."

Stone looked down at Muldoon.

Muldoon winked at him. "How's about a drink, big feller?"

"You lied to me, old man."

"Where's my drink?"

Stone realized Muldoon was a pathetic old drunkard who couldn't help himself, and he didn't have the heart to deny Muldoon what he so obviously craved. "Whiskey for my friend and me," Stone called out to Doreen.

"Be with you in a minute."

Doreen served the beer to a cowboy drinking alone at the other end of the bar. Along the far wall, a man in a striped shirt, wearing a derby hat, sat at a piano and plinked the keys. Doreen placed glasses and a bottle in front of Stone and Muldoon. She leaned over the bar, revealing the upper portion of her surging breasts, and looked Muldoon in the eye.

"You oughtta be ashamed of yourself, Muldoon."

"Meet my friend, John Stone."

She turned to Stone and smiled. "I'm Doreen Eckles," she said. "You new around here?"

"Just rode in."

"What brings you to Petie?"

Stone took out the picture of Marie and showed it to her. "Ever see her?"

"Who is she?"

"Friend of mine."

Doreen looked at the picture. "She don't look like nobody I ever seen."

"Muldoon said you were her."

"I don't look anything like her. Like I just told you, Muldoon'll do anything for a drink."

"Ain't that the truth," Muldoon agreed, a broad grin on his face.

Stone picked up the bottle and filled Muldoon's glass, while Muldoon stared transfixed at the amber liquid. Then Stone filled his own glass.

"To happy days," Stone said.

They touched glasses. Muldoon's hand quivered as he raised his whiskey to his lips and slurped like a dog. Stone took a swallow and let the whiskey burn its way down his throat. It was fairly smooth and had a sweet smoky taste, unlike the usual rotgut found on the frontier.

Muldoon drained his glass, then wiped his mouth with the back of his hand and placed his glass on the bar, looking at Stone with his puppy-dog eyes.

Stone pushed the bottle toward him. "Help yourself."

Muldoon eagerly reached for the bottle. Stone looked at Doreen, pouring whiskey at the other end of the bar. He hadn't looked at a woman for eight days, and she was a balm for his eyes. She glanced back at him and their eyes met for a few seconds. A silent communication passed between them, then she returned to her work. He turned around, leaning his back against the bar.

The piano player continued to play. Stone was struck by the tranquillity of the saloon. There were no fistfights, no shootings, no loud arguments. It was a civilized place, and he was able to relax. He thought he'd stay in Petie for a few days and clean up, then move on to the next town and find out if anybody there had seen Marie.

He remembered Mortimer, his horse, tied to the rail across the street. The horse was thirsty and hungry, and needed to be taken care of. Stone dropped a few coins on the bar.

"Got to leave," he said to Muldoon.

Stone walked erectly like a soldier toward the door, his stomach in and chest out, broad shoulders rolling slightly, spurs jangling.

"Come back anytime," said Doreen.

Stone touched his finger to the brim of his hat and pushed open the doors of the saloon, stepping onto the sidewalk. He crossed the street, pausing to let a wagon stacked high with hides pass by. The hides emitted the terrible odor of rotten meat, and Stone held his breath, then dashed toward his horse. He tightened the cinch under Mortimer's belly and climbed into the saddle.

"Sorry I kept you waiting, but there was something I had to do."

Stone and Mortimer headed toward the stable. Stone'd feed and water the horse, rub him down, and check into the nearest hotel for a bath and a shave. Then he'd have a meal at the best restaurant in Petie.

He rode down the center of the street, looking at the citizens of the town. Most were well dressed and well groomed, except for a few cowboys who looked like they'd been sleeping in their clothes. The ladies didn't appear overworked and worn out like most women on the frontier.

I think I'm going to like it here, Stone thought, feeling relaxed and content. The whiskey settled him down, and the peaceful ambiance of the town wrapped him in a warm glow. It'd be nice to take it easy for a few days in such a congenial place. He saw old men seated on benches, smoking pipes and cigarettes. Three women laughed in front of Brandon's Fine Jewelry. A little girl in a white dress skipped past the Acme Saloon.

Suddenly gunfire erupted in front of Stone, and Mortimer was so shocked he raised his front hooves high in the air. Stone turned in the direction of the shooting and saw men with bandannas over their faces running out of the Petie Savings Bank, firing pistols in all directions!

Women screamed hysterically and everyone dashed for cover. The robbers, carrying heavy saddlebags filled with money, continued to fire their pistols as they approached their horses, which were being held by one of their henchmen in front of the bank. A robber wearing a blue bandanna over his face saw Stone in the middle of the street and drew a bead on him.

Stone yanked out his pistol and fired. The robber dropped his pistol and staggered backward. Another robber was mounting his horse, swinging his leg over the saddle, and Stone fired again. The robber kept going over his saddle and slid down the other side, dropping to the ground and lying still.

The other robbers became aware of Stone firing at them. They aimed their pistols at him and let loose a barrage of bullets that whizzed around him and slammed into the dirt near Mortimer's hooves. Stone pulled his rifle out of its boot and leapt down from his saddle, running toward the far side of the street, diving behind a water trough.

Bullets whacked into the water trough, and water spurted out of the holes. Stone raised his head and saw some of the robbers climbing onto their horses, while the others continued to shoot at him, but he was an old soldier and it wasn't the first time in his life that he'd been under fire.

He levered the rifle and lined up the sights on one of the robbers who'd mounted a horse. He squeezed the trigger, the rifle barked, and the robber leaned to the side, dropping his pistol, falling to the ground. Another bullet struck the water trough, but Stone didn't flinch. He jacked the lever of his rifle, aimed at a robber on a horse, and squeezed the trigger again. The robber leaned forward and screamed, grasping his stomach with both his hands.

Stone worked the lever quickly. Four robbers were still alive on the far side of the street. One was mounted, ready to gallop out of town; the others had taken cover and were returning Stone's fire.

Stone glanced to his left and right. The street that was so crowded a few moments before had become deserted. People lay on the boardwalk, covering their heads with their hands. Children whimpered and dogs barked. Where the hell was the sheriff?

The robber on the horse attempted to gallop away. Stone led him with the barrel of his rifle and squeezed the trigger. The robber was knocked out of his saddle and he dropped his saddlebag, but his foot was caught in a stirrup and his horse dragged his lifeless body out of town.

A bullet whistled past Stone's ear, and he lowered his head behind the trough. A few feet away, a woman lying on the sidewalk looked at him with terror in her eyes. Stone knew he had a major advantage over the robbers on the far side of the street. They had pistols that were inaccurate at long distances, whereas his rifle could shoot the eye out of a squirrel at five hundred yards.

He raised his head and looked across the street. Three robbers lay on the sidewalk over there, and time was running out for them because they couldn't remain where they were indefinitely. Stone aimed his rifle at one of them, whose shoulder was showing behind a post that held up the roof in front of the bank. Stone's rifle exploded and kicked, and the robber went limp, his face dropping onto the boardwalk.

Now two robbers were left. They looked at each other and made a run for it, heading for their horses. One jumped into his saddle, and Stone shot him through the chest. The robber coughed blood and dropped his pistol, sagging to the side, falling to the ground.

The other robber landed in his saddle and wheeled his horse, putting the spurs to him, galloping away from the bank. Stone fired his rifle, and the hammer clicked. Something was wrong with the cartridge. Cursing, Stone ejected the bad cartridge and ran into the middle of the street. He dropped to one knee, raised the butt of the rifle to his shoulder, and took aim at the back of the robber riding furiously out of town.

The robber crouched low in his saddle, slapping the haunches of his horse with his reins. Stone took a deep breath, held it, and squeezed the trigger. His sights were lined up in the middle of the robber's back. The rifle fired and Stone became enveloped in gunsmoke. The robber jerked in his saddle and crouched even lower. Stone levered the rifle and prepared to fire again when he noticed the robber slipping out of his saddle. The robber tried desperately to hold on, clawing at his horse's mane, but his life was ebbing out of the hole in his left kidney. He toppled to the ground, rolled over a few times, and was still.

Stone got to his feet. Dead robbers were everywhere, and saddlebags full of money lay on the ground. It was like standing in the middle of a ghost town. Stone clicked the safety switch on his rifle and stood with his legs spread apart, the wide brim of his hat casting a shadow over his bearded face.

"Is it all over?" somebody asked.

"Looks that way," another person said.

People raised themselves off the boardwalks and stepped cautiously out of doorways, the men carrying rifles and pistols. Women adjusted their bonnets, and children held on to their mothers' skirts. Gradually the town came to life again, and a crowd formed around Stone, looking at him curiously.

A man in a suit walked out of the Petie Savings Bank, carrying a rifle, followed by two clerks wearing eyeshades. The man in the suit grinned broadly as he approached Stone.

"That was a helluva show you just put on," he said. "Who are you anyway?"

"My name's John Stone."

"I'm Clyde Akerson, and you just saved my bank over thirty thousand dollars. I'd like to buy you a drink."

"I've got to take my horse to the stable."

Akerson turned to the man behind him. "Take Mr. Stone's horse to the stable."

The man walked toward Mortimer, who was standing at the side of the street, not far from where Stone had left him. Akerson looked up at Stone. "Can we have that drink now?"

"Don't see any reason why not."

"Mr. Stone, I've never seen shooting like that in my life."

Akerson and Stone walked toward the Paradise Saloon, followed by a horde of townspeople. Children stood on benches and applauded as Stone walked past. Women gazed at him with wonderment in their eyes. Men he didn't know slapped him on the back and cheered. Stone still was slightly dazed by what had happened. It had all gone down so quickly.

They entered the saloon and walked toward the bar. Doreen still was behind the stick, and Muldoon was working on the bottle Stone had bought him.

"Drinks for the house!" Akerson shouted.

Doreen placed a bottle and two glasses in front of Stone and Akerson, then proceeded to set up the rest of the bar. Akerson poured whiskey into both the glasses, and Stone leaned his rifle against the bar.

Akerson was in his fifties, clean-shaven, with graying hair and a bald spot on top. Crow's-feet were around his eyes, and he had a gold tooth. A gold watch chain was extended across his paunch.

He raised his glass in the air. "To John Stone!" he shouted.

"To John Stone!" the crowd echoed.

Akerson touched his glass to Stone's and then other men pressed forward and clicked their glasses against his. Now that Stone was able to think clearly, he wondered why he'd bothered to get into a shootout with a bunch of robbers who'd outnumbered him. He supposed it was because one of them had made the mistake of taking a shot at him, and that had sent him into action almost before he knew what he was doing, because he was an old war dog at heart. If they hadn't shot at him, he would've left them alone.

The crowd cheered as he raised his glass and took a gulp of whiskey. The saloon was chock full of people, crowding around Stone, talking excitedly. It was a big party.

"What brings you to Petie, Mr. Stone?" Akerson asked him.

"I'm looking for somebody." He reached into his shirt pocket and took out the picture of Marie. "Ever see her?"

Akerson looked at the photograph. "Afraid not. Who is she?"

"Friend of mine."

"A lot of people in this town would've lost their life savings if it hadn't been for you, and my bank probably would've been busted. We're very grateful to you. Name it and it's yours."

"All I want is a hotel room, a bath, and a good hot meal."

"It's all on me, and anything else you want too. Where you coming from?"

"Long ways."

"I see you're wearing an old Confederate Army hat. What outfit were you with?"

"Third South Carolina Cavalry."

"Were you an officer?"

"Only a captain."

There was a commotion, and Stone turned around. Two men pushed their way through the boisterous crowd. One was fiftyish and stout, with a short wide beard and wearing a black hat with the narrow brim favored by businessmen in the East. The other was a clergyman wearing a black suit and a white collar, thin and severe-looking, with large ears.

"What's going on here?" said the stout man, approaching Akerson.

"May I present Captain John Stone," replied Akerson. "He just stopped a bank robbery single-handed. Captain Stone, may I present Martin Randlett, our mayor. And that's the Reverend Vernon Scobie, pastor of the Petie Church of God."

Stone shook hands with the two men, and Akerson explained in graphic detail how Stone had subdued the bank robbers. "It was an incredible display of marksmanship," Akerson said. "The man's got nerves of steel."

Mayor Randlett, the stout man in his fifties, looked up at Stone. "Sounds like you've saved us from some big trouble. Nothing's too good for you around here, Captain Stone."

"That's what I already told him," Akerson said.

"What're you doing in our town?" Mayor Randlett asked.

"Just passing through."

"You're not leaving us, if we can help it. We can use a man like you around here, can't we, gents?"

A roar went up from the crowd, and Akerson poured Stone another drink. The mayor slapped Stone on the back. "What's your line of work, Captain Stone?"

"I don't have a line of work."

"What do you do for a living?"

"Odd jobs."

"I'm sure we can find something suitable for you in our town. How'd you like to be deputy sheriff?"

"I don't think so."

"Why don't we have a seat and talk this over?"

Mayor Randlett pushed men with glasses in their hands aside as he made his way toward the table under the painting of naked women cavorting in the meadow. Akerson urged Stone to follow Mayor Randlett, and the Reverend Scobie brought up the rear. Akerson carried the bottle and placed it in the middle of the table as they all sat down. Only the Reverend Scobie was without a glass.

Stone rolled himself a cigarette. The other citizens crowded around, staring at him, guzzling whiskey and beer. Mayor

Randlett was seated next to Stone, who scraped a match on the underside of the table, lighting his cigarette.

"Why don't you want to be our new deputy sheriff?" Mayor Randlett asked.

"There's something that I've got to do," Stone replied.

"What is it?"

"It's personal."

Akerson nudged Stone in the ribs gently. "Does it have something to do with the picture of that girl you showed me?"

"That's right."

"What picture of what girl?" asked the mayor.

Stone took the picture of Marie out of his shirt pocket. "Ever see her?"

Mayor Randlett looked at Marie. "Don't believe so. Who is she?"

"We were supposed to get married, but when I got home after the war, she was gone. I'm looking for her."

"A lot of years have passed since the war ended. You're awfully persistent."

"I'll find her someday."

"A man's business is his own business," said the mayor, "but there comes a time in a man's life when he's got to face reality and think about settling down. This is a mighty fine town, Captain Stone. A man could make a good life for himself here, especially a man like you. We'll give you top pay, and you'll probably become sheriff here yourself after a while."

"Where's the sheriff you've got now?"

Mayor Randlett looked at Akerson. "Anybody seen Rawlins?"

"Not that I know of."

Mayor Randlett leaned toward Stone. "Between you and me and the fly on the wall, we wouldn't mind getting rid of our present sheriff, and you could replace him if you wanted the job. Maybe you ought to think twice before you turn the job down."

"Not interested," said Stone.

"Maybe you'll never find that girl."

"I'll find her."

"How're you fixed for money?"

"Not so well."

"Here's your chance to make an honest dollar. Why not try out the job? You might like it."

Stone thought about what Mayor Randlett said. He was low on money and would have to get a job sooner or later. Why not now?

"How much?" Stone asked.

"Two hundred a month, and we wouldn't even ask you to post bond."

That was good pay, substantially higher than what cowboys earned, and Stone had intended to get a job as a cowboy to replenish his sagging finances. Maybe he could work as deputy sheriff for a while until he got ahead of the game, and then he'd leave Petie, continuing his search for Marie.

"Could I try the job for a couple of weeks?"

"Try it for as long as you like."

"Let me think it over. I'll give you my answer in the morning."

2

DEKE CASEY SAT on the ground in the shade of Hawksridge Mountains, waiting for his men to return from the bank robbery in Petie.

He was the leader of an outlaw gang, and he'd planned the robbery in detail, after having visited Petie numerous times, mapping out locations, planning strategy, and even holding rehearsals out on the prairie.

Fifteen men were in his gang, including himself, and he'd chosen nine to stage the robbery. He hadn't wanted to use all his men, because he thought it'd be too many and they'd get in one another's way.

Casey was slim, with a long face and a thin mouth. He wore a dirty gray hat with a wide brim and a high crown with a crease down the middle. A cigarette dangled out of the corner of his mouth.

Nearby, a group of his men played poker, raising and calling one another, using pebbles for chips. Embers of their breakfast campfire sent a thin trail of smoke into the sky. A few members of the gang slept in the caves nearby.

They'd all been members of Bloody Bill Anderson's guerrilla cavalry during the war, fighting for the Confederacy, but mostly against civilians with Union sympathies. They'd left a trail of terror behind them, plundering, raping, committing massacres, burning entire towns to the ground, and they hadn't surrendered after the war. They'd just continued with what they'd been doing during the war, with Deke Casey as their leader.

Deke Casey wore a red and black checked shirt and a black leather vest. He took his watch out of a pocket in his vest and looked at the time. His men should've returned by now. He wondered if anything had gone wrong.

Anything could go wrong with a bank robbery, but he'd thought the bank in Petie would be easy. It was a peaceful town and the citizens weren't very vigilant because nothing bad ever happened there. Deke had got the sheriff out of the way by forging a note from one of the local ranchers, asking the sheriff to investigate the rustling of some cattle.

The sheriff was Buck Rawlins, an old gunfighter, but he was drinking heavily and didn't appear to be much of a threat anymore. Still, Casey had seen no point in tangling with Rawlins, so he'd devised the ruse to make sure he wouldn't be in town while the robbery was taking place.

Casey and his gang roamed the frontier, playing hit and run. They robbed banks, rustled cattle, held up stagecoaches, did anything that promised easy money. Sometimes they lived in fancy hotels and ate in the best restaurants, and mostly they camped in the open, as in the days when they rode with Bloody Bill Anderson. They were hard men who never hesitated to kill. Bitterness and hatred were in their hearts, and they felt they had the right to do whatever was necessary to maintain themselves as a free-roving fighting unit.

"Somebody's comin'," said Mike Chopak, a grizzled bear-like man, sitting at the card game with a pair of queens and a pair of fives in his hand.

Everybody dropped their cards and drew their guns. They moved behind boulders or dropped flat on the ground. Deke Casey took cover behind the trunk of the tree. His men probably were returning, but it could be Indians.

The cigarette dangled out of the corner of Deke Casey's mouth as he thumbed back the hammer of his Remington. The faint clatter of hoofbeats came to him, but it sounded like only one horse. He peered around the side of the tree, but couldn't see anything yet. Puffing the cigarette, he narrowed his snake eyes to slits and waited.

"It's Hurley," said Fritz Schuler, a blond man with long sideburns.

Schuler was closer to the canyon than the others, and had the best view. Casey eased the hammer of his Remington forward and dropped it into his holster. He stood next to the tree and hooked his thumbs in his belt as he watched Tom Hurley ride into view.

Hurley was a short man with a ratlike face, wearing leather chaps. He rode toward the campfire, pulled back on his reins, and climbed down from his saddle, a solemn expression on his face.

"It went bad," he said.

Casey and the others gathered around him. Hurley took off his hat, whacked it on his knee to get the dust out, and then put the hat back on his head.

"I was down the street from the bank when the boys went in," he said. "Everything looked good, the sheriff was out of town, there was no problems. Then all of a sudden this big guy on a horse comes ridin' down the middle of the street. The boys come out of the bank, carryin' the loot and shootin' at everythin' in sight, and Charlie Phelan decides to take a shot at the big guy. Well, the big guy quick-draws and shoots Charlie down. Then the big guy takes out his rifle, hides behind a water trough on the far side of the street, and picks off the boys one by one. They're all dead now, and the big guy is a hero. When I left town, they was throwin' a party for him in the Paradise Saloon."

Deke Casey couldn't believe his ears. "Are you tellin' me that one man killed everybody?"

"That's what I'm tellin' you."

A scowl came over Deke Casey's face as he chewed on the end of his cigarette. "Why didn't you do somethin'?"

"What the hell could I do?"

"Shoot the big guy."

"He would've got me just like he got the others. He was a dead shot. You wouldn't've done no better."

Casey sucked smoke from his wet cigarette. "Who the hell is this big guy?"

"Well, after it was all over, the mayor set up the bar at the Paradise, and I went over to see what was goin' on. I had me a drink, mindin' my own business, askin' a few questions. All I could find out was the big guy had just rode into town that mornin', and nobody knows where he come from. His name is John Stone."

Stone stood barefooted in front of the mirror, scraping a straight razor across his cheek. A towel was wrapped around his waist, and on the bed lay new jeans and a new shirt, courtesy of Caldwell's General Store. A bottle of premium bourbon sat on the dresser, courtesy of Petie Spirits and Liquors, and next to the bourbon were boxes of cartridges for his pistols and rifles, courtesy of Main Street Shooters Supplies.

Stone had taken his first bath in nearly two weeks, and the tub near his bed was still filled with dirty water. His room was on the top floor of the Olympia Hotel, with a view of Main Street below him. Last time he'd looked out the window, he'd seen a bunch of kids on the far side of the street, looking up at him.

He'd become the local hero, and still hadn't got used to it yet. Usually he rode into towns and nobody paid any attention to him. He had to work for every bite of food and every drink of whiskey he got, but now everybody was buying things for him.

It was a welcome change, and he'd always liked luxury. He'd grown up as the son of a rich man, and had spent his days hunting and fishing, and his nights at parties. Life had become more austere when he attended West Point, and during the war he'd been an officer and a gentleman.

Since the war he'd been just another saddle tramp, sleeping under the stars more often than not, usually low on cash, frequently hungry, often lonely. The frontier had been a shock at first, because there was no law in most places. A man had to learn to take care of himself, and Stone soon learned that his best friends were his loaded guns. He had a slight advantage because he'd hunted since he was a small boy, and was a good shot. His marksmanship had improved during the war, and he still practiced regularly, every chance he got.

Stone finished shaving and washed the surplus lather from his face. Looking in the mirror, he examined his weather-beaten face. He had an aquiline nose, strong jaw, and prominent cheekbones, all visible now that his growth of beard was gone. His body was heavily muscled and his stomach was flat, with a few scars.

He put on his new clothes, and they smelled clean and fresh. His jeans were dark blue, his shirt was red, and they'd given him another black bandanna. He pulled on his boots, dropped his knife into the sheath sewn into his right boot, and buckled on his gunbelts. Then he picked his hat off the peg and reshaped the crown with his fingers.

He knew he should get a new hat, but couldn't give up his old one. He'd worn it through the war, and it was like an old friend. Smudged and discolored, it had character, in his opinion. You could see where he'd torn off the Confederate Army insignia, but it still held its shape pretty well and kept the rain and sun off him.

He put the hat on and looked at himself again in the mirror. It was nice to be clean again, living in pleasant surroundings for a change. He'd decided to take the job as deputy sheriff for a while, to build up his cash reserves. Then he'd resume his search for Marie.

He lifted her picture from the dresser and looked at it. She'd lived on the next plantation, and they'd grown up almost as brother and sister, until they grew older and things became serious. She was the only woman he'd ever loved, and he could never love anybody else. She was all he wanted in the world.

He dropped the picture into his shirt pocket and left the hotel room, descending the stairs to the lobby. People called his name and waved to him as he crossed the lobby, heading toward the front door. He stepped onto the sidewalk, and the kids across the street ran toward him, gathering around, gazing at him with admiration.

He smiled at them, tipped his hat to a lady, and walked in long strides down the street toward the Diamond Restaurant.

Sheriff Buck Rawlins approached the other end of town, riding his Appaloosa. He was six feet tall, had a black mustache, and wore a black hat with a wide flat brim and a flat crown. He was in a bad mood, because he'd just gone on a wild goose chase.

He'd received a note from the Double M Ranch, asking him to go out there to investigate some cattle rustling, but when he got there, the owner of the Double M, Phineas Mathers, had told him he'd sent no such note and wasn't having any problems with rustlers. Rawlins showed him the note, and Mathers said it wasn't even his handwriting.

Sheriff Rawlins's lips were set in a grim line as he rode down the main street of town, heading for his office. Somebody had played a trick on him, but he wasn't surprised. He knew he wasn't the most popular man in town, and in fact he had many enemies. He'd cleaned up the town in the old days, risking his life frequently in shootouts with drunken cowboys on a spree, bandits, and assorted hard cases, but now the townspeople didn't have much use for him anymore. He knew what they were saying behind his back, that he was getting old and he drank too much. Well, forty-six wasn't old, and everybody else in town took a drink now and then, so why shouldn't he? They also complained about his manners, but he was a lawman, not a dandy from the East with a perfumed handkerchief and poems for the ladies. He could still outshoot anybody in town, and that was all that mattered.

He stopped in front of his office, tethered his horse to the rail, and climbed onto the sidewalk. He looked to his left and right, and the town was quiet, people going about their business as always. He'd seen Petie grow from a rollicking little frontier settlement to the largest town in the territory.

He opened the door to the office and saw Abner Pritchard, his clerk, seated at the desk near the left wall, doing paperwork. The jail in back held a few drunks. Rawlins hung his hat on the peg and sat behind his desk in the middle of the room.

"Anything happen when I was gone?"

Pritchard was an emaciated man with a sunken chest, wearing a green visor and suspenders to hold up his pants. "You might be getting yourself a new deputy sheriff."

"What the hell are you talking about?"

Pritchard told him about the bank robbery, and how it was stopped cold by a stranger named John Stone. "He shot down all eight of the crooks," Pritchard said. "I didn't see it, but those who did said it was a helluva show."

Sheriff Rawlins's brow was furrowed as he opened the side drawer of his desk and pulled out his glass and a bottle of whiskey. He filled the glass half full and took a swig. His black hair was parted slightly to the left and combed flat, and his hollowed cheeks gave him a saturnine appearance. His jaw looked like it had been carved from a block of granite.

"So anyways," Pritchard said, "Mayor Randlett offered Stone the job of deputy sheriff, and Stone's supposed to tell him yes or no."

"He shouldn't've offered anybody the job of deputy sheriff without talkin' with me first. You see this Stone feller?"

"Akerson set up the bar over at the Paradise, and I went over for a quick drink. Stone's a big, strong-looking galoot with shoulders out to here." Pritchard held up his hands to indicate the size of Stone's shoulders, and they appeared wider than Sheriff Rawlins's. "Other than that he looked like a bum."

"John Stone prob'ly ain't his real name. He might be on the dodge. I'll have to check the wanted posters."

"Mind if I go out for a bite?"

"Don't take too long."

Pritchard tore off his green visor and walked out of the office. Sheriff Rawlins took another drink of whiskey and thought about the bank holdup. He surmised that the forged note must've been sent to him to get him out of town while the holdup was going on, but somehow John Stone had been in the right place at the right time.

"Killed all eight of them," Rawlins muttered, because he often spoke to himself. "Wonder how he did that?" He gulped more whiskey and lit a long, thin black stogie, smoke swirling around his head. "They shouldn't've offered him the deputy's job until they checked with me. I'm only the sheriff around here, after all. I haveta find out what's goin' on from my goddamned clerk."

Sheriff Rawlins raised the glass to his lips again. He felt himself getting angry. Cursing the town and its citizens, he drained the glass and let the whiskey burn all the way down to his soul.

Deke Casey sat against a rock, whittling a stick with the long knife he carried in a sheath on his belt. His men were lying around nearby, not playing poker anymore. They were all in a rotten mood over the massacre of their henchmen in Petie.

Casey couldn't understand how such a setback could take place. It didn't make sense that one man could stop eight experienced gunfighters who also had long combat records. *Who in the hell was John Stone?* he wondered. Hurley had described Stone, but Stone didn't remind Hurley of any outlaw or gunfighter he'd ever heard of. *Must be somebody new,* he thought.

Casey knew his men expected him to do something about the killings. He couldn't let Stone get away with sending eight of his best men to boot hill. Casey and his men lived by the old biblical code, an eye for an eye and a tooth for a tooth. Stone would have to be killed. He couldn't be permitted to get away with shooting down eight men from Bloody Bill Anderson's old outfit.

"Chopak—get over here!" he shouted.

Mike Chopak, nearly as wide as he was tall, picked himself up from the ground and walked toward Casey. The sleeves of his shirt were torn off, revealing huge bicep muscles, and the muscle on the left bicep showed a blurred crude tattoo of a skull.

"Take a man with you and ride into Petie," Casey said. "Find out where this John Stone lives and what his routine is. Get as much information on him that you can, and then come back and report to me."

Chopak nodded. He turned around and walked back to the others. "Ramsay," he said. "Let's go."

Fred Ramsay raised himself from the ground and spit a gob of tobacco juice out the corner of his mouth. He was tall as Chopak, but built like a stiletto. His tight-fitting shirt was fraying at the collar and around his wrists. He and Chopak walked wordlessly toward their horses.

Casey watched them saddle their mounts. He didn't know John Stone, but hated him with a slow simmering passion. Casey and his men were low on cash and supplies, and they'd have to do something soon to replenish the larder.

But they lived by their own harsh code of justice, and first they had to pay back John Stone for killing their comrades.

John Stone sat by himself at a table in the Diamond Restaurant, eating a large wedge of apple pie. He'd just finished a steak dinner with all the trimmings, and his appetite was satisfied. It was his first good meal in eight days. Trail food cooked over open campfires, or sometimes not cooked at all, could get awfully boring.

It was a small restaurant with ten tables and red and white checkered tablecloths. He was aware of men and women at other tables looking at him and talking about him. It made him feel conspicuous and uneasy, after so many solitary days alone on the prairie. He finished his pie and sipped a cup of hot black coffee.

"I'll take the check," he said to his waitress when she passed his table.

"There won't be no check, Captain Stone," she said. "It's all taken care of."

"By who?"

"Mr. Thomaston."

Thomaston was the owner of the Diamond Restaurant, and had greeted Stone like a long-lost relative when Stone had entered. Now Thomaston was bustling in and out of the kitchen, supervising the activities of his busy establishment. He wore a suit and a long mustache with upturned points.

Stone threw a few coins on the table for the waitress, and arose, picking his hat off the peg. Thomaston saw him and rushed over, an ingratiating smile on his perspiring face.

"Hope you enjoyed your meal, Captain."

"I did enjoy it, thank you."

Thomaston beamed as he watched Stone walk toward the door. It would be good for business if word got around that Captain John Stone patronized the Diamond Restaurant.

Stone stepped onto the sidewalk and placed his hat upon his head. He felt strong, clean, and ready to go to work. He'd decided during lunch that he'd take the deputy sheriff job, and there was no point waiting to tell Mayor Randlett. He thought he'd go to the mayor now and accept the job.

"Good afternoon, Captain Stone."

A stout woman with pudgy cheeks was addressing him. He'd never seen her before in his life, but he tipped his hat and said, "Good afternoon."

She smiled broadly, showing teeth like a horse's. "I'm Mabel Billings and I'm president of the Ladies Auxiliary at the church.

I'd like to invite you personally to attend services with us on Sunday morning. Reverend Scobie preaches a fine sermon."

"I've met the reverend, and I'll attend the services if I'm able. Thank you for inviting me, ma'am."

"I look forward to seeing you, Captain. It'll be about time that a lawman in this town went to church."

"Could you tell me where I might find Mayor Randlett?"

"I imagine he's in his office, down the street on the right."

Mrs. Billings waddled past him and Stone crossed the street thinking that he might actually attend church on Sunday. It was a nice thing to do, and he believed in God in some vague way. He'd gone to church every Sunday when he'd grown up, and it had become a habit with him, although he knew he was a sinner; he'd done a lot of things that he supposed God wouldn't approve of, but a man had to survive somehow. Religion was one thing, and the real world something else entirely.

On the other side of the street, Stone heard a guitar being strummed, and the guitar was badly out of tune. Ahead of him, seated on a bench in front of the blacksmith shop, was Toby Muldoon, singing a sad old cowboy tune drunkenly, tapping his foot on the sidewalk to keep up the beat.

Muldoon looked up as Stone approached. His melancholy expression transformed suddenly into a grin that showed his toothless gums. "Well hello there, Cap'n. What's up?"

"I'm on my way to the mayor's office."

"What for?"

"He offered me the job of deputy sheriff, and I decided to take it."

Muldoon's expression grew serious again. He tapped the bench next to him. "Have a seat."

Stone sat down. Muldoon looked to the left and right conspiratorially, and said in a low voice, "Watch out for Sheriff Rawlins. He ain't a-gonna like you, and he ain't nobody to fool with. When he gits drunk he gits mean. Saw somebody draw on him once, and Rawlins shot him before the fool even got his gun out of its holster. So you be careful, you understand?"

"I've got to see the mayor. What can you tell me about him?"

"Owns a good piece of this town and a big ranch west of here, the Circle J. He's a fancy lawyer too, works out of his office down the street here. Got a real pretty daughter, sweet as sugar, his only child, his wife died a few years back. You'll like his daughter, Jennifer's her name. Makes me wish I was young again. How's about a drink?"

"You drink too much, Muldoon."

"Don't tell me how to live, Cap'n. I been around too long, and I'm too old to change now."

Stone arose from the bench and handed Muldoon a few coins. Then he headed for Randlett's office, towering over most of the people he passed, and the sidewalk shook slightly whenever his boots came down. He passed a bakery, a Chinese laundry, and a ladies dress shop. Then he saw a sign that said:

Martin Randlett
Attorney at Law

He opened the door and stepped inside an office. A beautiful young redhead sat behind the desk directly in front of him. Stone took off his hat.

"I'd like to see Mayor Randlett, if he's available."

"Who shall I say is calling?"

"John Stone."

She smiled. "Oh, so you're the one everybody's talking about. I'm Jennifer Randlett, the mayor's daughter. How do you do."

She stood behind the desk and held out her hand, and it felt like a dove. She had green eyes and smooth creamy skin, and her hair was like fire.

"I'll get my father."

She turned around and walked toward the door behind her. She was slim-waisted and had nice curves in the right places, moving with a graceful swaying gait. Stone fingered the brim of his hat with both his hands as she opened the door and entered the next room. He'd seen a lot of attractive women in his life, and in the old days, before the war, he'd been acquainted with some of the most renowned belles of the South. Jennifer Randlett would rank with the prettiest of them, and even with Marie Higgins, who'd been quite a famous beauty herself.

A few moments later Mayor Randlett emerged from his office, followed by his daughter. "You look like a new man," he said to Stone. "Glad you stopped by." He placed his arm around Jennifer's shoulders. "I guess you met my daughter. What can I do for you?"

"I've decided to accept your offer."

"I was hoping you would, and we might as well tie everything up quickly before you change your mind. Why don't you go down to the sheriff's office and wait for me. I'll be there with the Reverend Scobie in about a half hour."

Stone turned to leave, but Mayor Randlett raised his hand.

"I think you made the right decision," he said. "This is a growing town, and you can grow with it. People here like you and want you to stay. There's no limit to what a man like you can accomplish in a town like this."

"I don't want to misrepresent myself," Stone told him. "My plan is to work here for exactly one month, and then move on."

"Maybe you'll change your mind about that, Captain."

"I doubt it, sir."

Stone left the office and walked down the street toward the sheriff's office. He was thinking about Jennifer Randlett, how she'd stood calmly at her father's side, measuring Stone, curiosity in her eyes and a faint smile on her lips.

Muldoon had been right: Stone liked her. He didn't hardly know her, but she seemed decent and wholesome, and he'd always been attracted to women like her. Marie had been the same way, the kind of woman a man could trust. Muldoon said Jennifer was Mayor Randlett's only daughter, which meant she'd inherit all he owned someday. She'd be quite a catch for some lucky cowboy.

He came to the sheriff's office. A few wanted posters were tacked to the bulletin board beside it, and the sign on the door said:

BUCK RAWLINS
Sheriff of Petie

Stone opened the door and stepped inside the office. A cadaverous man wearing a green visor sat behind the desk to his left, and a craggy-faced man with a mustache, smoking a stogie and wearing a badge on the lapel of his frock coat, sat behind the desk to his right.

"Sheriff Rawlins?" Stone asked the latter man.

"What do you want?" Sheriff Rawlins replied.

"I'm John Stone, your new deputy."

Sheriff Rawlins looked up at Stone through hooded eyes, and Stone could smell whiskey. There was silence in the office for a few moments, then Sheriff Rawlins picked up a piece of paper and read it, ignoring Stone.

Stone had never been a lawman before, and wasn't sure of exactly how to proceed. He'd been chased by lawmen, and had been in jail once, but that was all he knew about it.

Stone looked around, saw a chair underneath the rifle rack, and sat on it. He took out his bag of tobacco and rolled himself a cigarette, then placed it in between his lips and lit it up.

Sheriff Rawlins glanced at him. "I didn't say you could smoke."

"You didn't say I couldn't."

"If you want to smoke in my office, you ask me first."

"Like hell I will."

Sheriff Rawlins turned red, and Stone could see the ends of his black mustache quivering.

"I don't think we're gonna git along," Sheriff Rawlins said.

"That's up to you."

"I guess you think you're real special in this town, after what you done, but I ain't impressed like everybody else because I know better. If them bank robbers had been any good they would've shot yer fuckin' head off, but instead they was just a bunch of bunglers and fumblers who let themselves git killed by you. Christ, my clerk Pritchard here prob'ly could've handled them, and he can't even hardly see straight. You're gonna find out, Sonny Jim, that this job ain't as easy as you think. For all I know, you're a wanted man yerself. Where you from?"

"South Carolina."

"I didn't ask you where you was born. I asked you what town you was in before you come here."

"Some town north of here. Don't remember the name. Wasn't there that long." Stone knew very well what town he'd been in, but didn't want to mention it because that was the town in which he'd been in jail.

"You look like an owlhoot to me."

Stone shrugged, then took a long draw on his cigarette,

blowing the smoke out the corner of his mouth. Pritchard sat across the room at his desk, in a mild state of shock. He'd never heard anybody talk back to Rawlins before. Everybody in Petie was afraid of Rawlins, because of his bad temper and fast gun.

Sheriff Rawlins stared at Stone. "Are you an owlhoot?"

Stone leaned back in his chair, crossed his legs, and puffed his cigarette.

"I just asked you something," Rawlins said menacingly.

"I don't answer stupid questions."

Rawlins turned red again. He was tempted to whip out his Colt and put a hole in John Stone, but this wasn't the time or the place, and besides, there was something about Stone's manner that made him think twice about it. Stone was like a big mountain lion relaxing in the chair across the room, and Rawlins knew that a mountain lion could go from complete repose to a total all-out attack in a split second. Sheriff Rawlins couldn't help feeling respect for a man he couldn't intimidate, because he was accustomed to intimidating everybody he met, but that didn't make him hate Stone any less.

Sheriff Rawlins returned his eyes to the correspondence in front of him. Across the room, Pritchard's pen scratched on a piece of paper. Stone puffed his cigarette and looked around the office. Wanted posters were tacked to the walls, an American flag hung limply from the top of a pole, and a picture of Bobby Lee was mounted on the wall above the cot.

The door to the office opened, and Mayor Randlett entered, followed by the Reverend Vernon Scobie, who was carrying a black Bible.

"Afternoon, Sheriff," Mayor Randlett said, smiling in a friendly manner.

Sheriff Rawlins looked up at him and scowled darkly.

"Guess you met your new deputy."

"I never asked for no deputy."

"We thought you could use one—take some of the work off your shoulders. Captain Stone here's a good man. He'll be a real help to you."

"Seem to me I should have some say in who's hired to be my deputy."

"We didn't think you'd have any objection to Captain Stone

giving you a hand," Mayor Randlett said. "After what he did today, the town council and I thought he'd be ideal. Surely you don't object to having Captain Stone as your deputy?"

"What the hell's all this *captain* stuff? What's he a captain of?"

"He was a captain of cavalry for the Confederacy during the war."

"The war's been over a long time."

"But we don't forget, do we, Sheriff? You were a sergeant in the Confederate infantry, so you and Captain Stone were comrades in arms. That'll give you something in common. If you don't have any objection to Captain Stone becoming your deputy, Reverend Scobie will swear him in right now."

"Do what you want," Sheriff Rawlins said gruffly.

"Captain Stone, will you step over here please?"

Stone stubbed out his cigarette in an ashtray and sauntered across the room to where Mayor Randlett and the Reverend Scobie were standing.

"Place your left hand on the Bible, please, and raise your right hand in the air."

Stone did as he was told, and the Reverend Scobie opened his mouth. His Adam's apple bobbed up and down as he intoned gravely: "Do you, John Stone, swear to uphold the laws of the town of Petie, to the best of your ability, so help you God?"

"I do," said Stone.

Now it was Mayor Randlett's turn to speak. "Pursuant to the authority vested in me by the charter of the town of Petie, I hereby appoint you deputy sheriff of the town of Petie, for an indeterminate period, beginning today."

Mayor Randlett smiled, and the Reverend Scobie tucked the Bible underneath his arm. He looked more like an undertaker than a minister of God.

"Congratulations," said Mayor Randlett. "I'm sure you'll do a good job."

"I'll try my best," Stone replied.

"That's all we can ask." Mayor Randlett pulled a tin badge out of his vest pocket and pinned it on Stone's shirt. "Just had this made up at the blacksmith's place. It's a little rough around the edges, but it'll do. Good luck to you."

The Reverend Scobie shook his hand and wished him well. Pritchard remained rooted to his chair, writing with his pen as if nothing unusual was taking place, and Sheriff Rawlins shuffled through papers on his desk, also showing a lack of interest.

"Well," said Mayor Randlett, "we've got to be on our way. Lots to do, you know. I'll leave you here with Sheriff Rawlins, who'll explain your duties."

Mayor Randlett left the office, followed by the Reverend Scobie. Stone turned around and faced Sheriff Rawlins, who'd pulled an old newspaper from his bottom drawer and was reading it.

"What're my duties?" Stone asked.

Sheriff Rawlins glanced up at him. "You'll have the shift from eight at night till eight in the morning, seven days a week, but you're always on call. You can start at eight tonight."

Sheriff Rawlins raised the paper and covered his face. Stone stood in front of him silently for a few moments, waiting for more instructions, and realized he wasn't going to get any more. He reached out and pushed the paper down until he could see Rawlins's face again.

"What does a deputy sheriff do?" Stone asked.

Sheriff Rawlins glowered at him. "You figger it out."

Mike Chopak and Fred Ramsay rode down the main street of Petie, trying to appear casual, as if they weren't outlaws. They'd never been in the town before, and no one knew who they were. They passed the Petie Savings Bank and looked at each other significantly, because that's where their pals had been gunned down by John Stone. Angling their horses to the other side of the street, they came to the stop in front of the Paradise Saloon.

They tied up their horses and went inside. Nobody paid any special attention to them, because strangers often showed up in town, on their way to other places. Cowboys were hired and fired at the various ranches in the territory, and there were always new faces to see. Chopak and Ramsay weren't on any wanted posters in that part of the frontier, as far as they knew, and made their way to the bar, confident they were safe.

"What's your pleasure, gents?" asked Doreen Eckles.

"Whiskey," said Chopak.

Doreen placed two glasses and a bottle in front of them. Chopak filled the glasses half full, and he and Ramsay took a drink. They looked strange together, because Chopak was so wide and Ramsay so slim. Chopak's arms were enormous, and it was hard not to notice them, because he'd torn the sleeves off his shirt.

Chopak and Ramsay sipped their whiskey and turned around, looking at the men playing cards at the tables. The saloon had a festive air and most of the people were well dressed. Chopak and Ramsay felt out of place. Their clothes were dirty and they hadn't bathed for several days.

There was an empty table near the wall, and Chopak motioned with his head toward it. He picked up his glass and the bottle, and threaded his way past the other tables, heading for the empty one. He bumped people a few times, and had to say, "Excuse me," because he was so wide.

He came to the table and sat down, his massive haunches spilling over the seat of his chair. Ramsay sat opposite him and pulled his hat low over his eyes so no one could get a good look at his face. He leaned toward Chopak.

"I hate these fuckin' people," he muttered.

Chopak winked, reaching for his bag of tobacco. He didn't like ordinary citizens either, and was tempted to draw his gun and start shooting at them, just for the hell of it.

He liked a good massacre, and had participated in a few during his career. The biggest and best was in Lawrenceville, Kansas, which he and the other boys under Bloody Bill Anderson had burned to the ground, shooting all the men, raping the women.

He'd love to do the same thing in Petie and see the smug, self-satisfied faces all around him covered with blood, begging for mercy, shaking in their boots. He spat into the nearby cuspidor and scratched his armpit. It was a nice thing to think about. These people looked like they could use a good dose of reality.

A man wearing a derby pushed open the doors of the saloon and stepped boldly inside. "We got us a new deputy sheriff!" he shouted. "The mayor just swore him in!"

A cheer went up in the saloon, and a few of the men whistled. The man in the derby walked to the bar and ordered a drink. He held his glass in the air and yelled, "Here's to Deputy Sheriff John Stone!"

The men cheered again. Chopak looked at Ramsay, his face blank but his eyes sparkling with animosity. Ramsay nodded.

At the next table, four men played poker. "Anybody tries to rob the bank again," one of them said, "and John Stone'll show 'em a thing or two."

"He's one tough son of a bitch," another man at the table replied. "Outlaws'd better steer clear of Petie, if they wanna go on breathin'."

Chopak's knuckles went white around the glass in his hand.

John Stone entered his hotel room and locked the door behind him. Sitting on the bed, he pulled off his high-topped black boots. He wanted to get some rest, because it was going to be a long night.

He unstrapped his guns, took off his clothes, and splashed water on his face. Then he lay on top of the bed, placing the palms of his hands behind his head and staring at the white paint on the ceiling.

Sheriff Rawlins had given him the dirty end of the stick, and Stone wasn't too happy about it. Frontier towns were at their worst during the night, when men got their drunkest, starting fights, shooting at each other, beating up their wives.

Stone wasn't tired, but somehow had to get some sleep in preparation for the night. He knew from experience in war that a man wasn't at his best when he was tired. His timing would be off, and that could cost his life.

Rawlins hadn't told him anything about what the job required, but Stone had been in many frontier towns and knew generally how lawmen functioned. The good ones roamed their towns, showing their badges and guns, and stepped into the middle of trouble if it came up. The bad ones hid someplace and hoped someone else would handle the trouble.

Stone wasn't about to hide and let somebody else handle the trouble. He'd been a conscientious officer during the war and always had taken his duties seriously. That's the way he was raised by his parents, and that's how they'd trained him at West Point. He wasn't about to change now.

The sounds of the street outside his window caught his attention. He heard hoofbeats, the voices of men, the laughter of women. All those people were depending upon him for protection, and he wondered whether he'd put himself in over his head.

The townspeople thought he was a hero, because he'd stopped the bank robbery, but he knew he'd done no great deed. A determined man with a rifle had superior firepower over anybody with pistols at a distance, and it would've been hard for him to lose. Another factor was that he'd taken the bank robbers by surprise, and the element of surprise was always a tremendous advantage. Jeb Stuart and Wade Hampton had taught him that in the war, and he'd never forgotten it.

Somehow sleep wouldn't come. It was too early in the day, and he was accustomed to sleeping at night. He thought of Jennifer Randlett working in her father's office. She certainly was lovely, and the memory of her made him feel warm all over.

She'd looked at him with more than casual interest, but he was engaged to Marie, and that bond could never be broken. He'd been tempted by other women in the past, but he'd never given in. It was one of the few things he was proud of, along with his service in the war and the times he'd helped people in need.

He punched up the pillow and tried to get comfortable, but somehow nothing worked. Rolling over onto his stomach, he grit his teeth and tried to force himself to fall asleep, but no matter what he did he remained awake, wondering what would happen to him on his first night as deputy sheriff of Petie.

3

STONE ROLLED OUT of bed at seven-thirty and touched his feet to the floor. He hadn't slept at all, had a mild headache, and felt irritable. He splashed water on his face, rolled a cigarette, and put on his clothes.

Lifting his shirt off the back of the chair, he looked at the badge. It was a crude lopsided star, cut hastily out of a thin piece of tin. DEPUTY SHERIFF was written across it, the words engraved with a hammer and a nail, dot by dot.

He put on the shirt and buttoned it up, then strapped on his two gunbelts. He'd learned long ago that two pistols were better than one, providing six extra shots without reloading, and that could spell the difference between life and death when bullets were flying around.

He inserted his knife into the sheath inside his boot, because a man never knew when he might need six inches of sharp steel. Then he placed his hat on his head and pulled the brim low over his eyes. Checking himself in the mirror, he couldn't help smiling. He'd never realized that someday he'd be a lawman.

He left the hotel and walked down the street toward the sheriff's office. Everyone he passed said hello to him, and he tipped his hat to the ladies. The sun was sinking toward the horizon on the west side of town, and the buildings cast long shadows. He walked past the Paradise Saloon and heard the piano tinkling inside. He was tempted to go in and have a drink, but thought he'd wait until later.

It was strange to think that he was protector of the town. If any problems cropped up, he was supposed to straighten them out although he knew nothing about law, and Sheriff Rawlins had given him no guidelines. Somehow he'd have to make up his own law as he went along.

He came to the sheriff's office and tried the doorknob, but it was locked. Pritchard had given him a ring of keys, so he tried them in the lock until one of them turned. He opened the door and entered the office, which smelled of tobacco smoke and whiskey. Leaving the door open, he lit a kerosene lamp and wondered where to put it. He had no desk of his own so decided to use Pritchard's desk for the time being. He placed the lamp on Pritchard's desk and sat behind it, pushing his hat to the back of his head.

He wondered what to do. *Maybe I should've bought a newspaper.* He took out his guns, made sure they were loaded, and stuffed them back into his holsters. Then he rolled a cigarette and lit it up. A faint breeze rustled the papers on Pritchard's desk, and it was quiet outside in the street except for the sound of hoofbeats as a man on a horse rode by.

It's a peaceful night so far, he said to himself. *Let's hope it stays that way.*

Seated on a bench in front of a cobbler's shop on the far side of the street were Mike Chopak and Fred Ramsay, passing a bottle of whiskey back and forth between them.

"So that's John Stone," Chopak said. "He don't look like so much to me."

"He's awful big," replied Ramsay, pulling a thread out of his fraying sleeve.

"Nobody's bigger than a bullet. I think we ought to take him down ourselves."

"Don't get no crazy ideas. Casey told us to find all we can about him and then go back to camp."

"Why waste time?" Chopak asked. "When it gets dark, I'll

just come up behind him and put a bullet in his head."

"I don't think you should try to take him on your own," Ramsay told him. "That's not the way Casey wants to play it."

Chopak turned to him and narrowed his small eyes. "I'm not gonna take him on my own, because you're gonna help me. You ain't afraid of this galoot, are you?"

"Hell no, I ain't afraid."

"He killed some good men, and he ain't gittin' away with it. We'll fix him later, you and me. These people around here might think he's a big hero, but he ain't gonna be much when he's lyin' on the ground with a bullet in his head."

Chopak turned toward the sheriff's office again. He saw a scrawny old man shuffling down the sidewalk on the far side of the street, carrying a guitar. The old man stopped in front of the door to the sheriff's office, straightened his back, and threw his left foot forward, staggering into the office.

Stone was looking at a wanted poster tacked to the wall when he heard footsteps behind him. He turned around and saw Toby Muldoon.

"Thought I'd stop by to see if you needed any help," Muldoon said. "How's it goin'?"

"Been pretty quiet so far."

"Well, if you need any help, you know who to call." Muldoon drew a rusty old pistol from his holster and waved it menacingly in the air. "I may not look like much, and I know I'm just an old goddamned drunk, but I ain't never run away from a fight in me life!"

Stone held up his hand. "Put that thing away before you shoot somebody."

"I won't shoot anybody, Cap'n. Hell, the damn thing ain't even loaded, and if it was loaded, it prob'ly wouldn't work anyway."

Just then the pistol fired, and a bullet went crashing into the ceiling. An expression of astonishment came over Muldoon's face. He looked at the smoking barrel of the gun.

"Now how'd that happen?" he asked.

"I think you'd better put it in your holster."

Muldoon nodded, dropping the gun into his holster, but his aim was off and the gun dropped to the floor, where it explod-

~ed again, shooting a bullet into the wall next to a filing cabinet.

"Damn!" said Muldoon. "Must be somethin' wrong with that gun."

"I don't think there's anything wrong with the gun, Muldoon. It seems to be working perfectly fine." Stone moved in quick strides toward Muldoon, picked up the gun, and placed it in Muldoon's holster. "Leave it in there, okay?"

Muldoon grinned. "Lend me some money so's I can buy me a drink, okay, pardner? When I come into my own, I'll pay you back."

If Stone gave Muldoon money, he'd just be contributing to his drunkenness, and if he denied him, it would be mean. Stone gave Muldoon a few coins.

"That's all for today," Stone said sternly.

"When I fust set eyes on you yesterday, I said to meself, 'There's a good man.' "

Muldoon walked out of the sheriff's office. Stone sat behind Pritchard's desk and looked up at the bullet hole in the ceiling. Then he turned to the bullet hole in the wall. *My first night on the job, and I let a drunk shoot up the sheriff's office.*

Stone's stomach rumbled, and he realized he hadn't had dinner yet. Putting on his hat, he walked outside and locked the door to the sheriff's office. He noticed two men sitting on the bench across the street, and recalled that they'd been there when he'd unlocked the sheriff's office after he'd first come on duty.

He didn't think anything special about the two men, but the fact of their existence registered in his mind. As a former army officer, he'd been trained to notice details.

He walked up the street toward the Diamond Restaurant, and two pairs of eyes observed his every movement.

"Let's go," said Chopak.

"You ain't gonna try to kill him now, are you?" asked Ramsay.

"First chance I git," Chopak replied.

The town of Petie consisted of a main street and several side streets. Residents lived in rooming houses, the hotel, or private homes. Some of the private homes on the outskirts of town were ramshackle affairs with sagging roofs and lopsided windows, and others were quite large and well constructed, freshly painted, with spacious yards, balconies, and porches.

The largest house in town was a white mansion with two neo-Georgian columns in front, two stories high, at the top of a hill in the best section. It was owned by Mayor Randlett, who lived in it with his daughter and numerous servants.

As Stone made his way toward the Diamond Restaurant, Mayor Randlett was seated in his dining room, finishing the soup course of his dinner. He was accompanied by his daughter, Jennifer; Clyde Akerson, manager of the Petie Savings Bank, of which Randlett was majority stockholder; and Marjorie Akerson, Clyde Akerson's wife, who wore an ill-fitting mail-order black wig, due to a disease that had caused her to lose all her hair when she was a little girl.

They were talking about John Stone.

"He's just what this town needs," Mayor Randlett said, pushing away his empty bowl of soup. "The days of men like Buck Rawlins are over. Rawlins was all right at the beginning when there was a killing nearly every day, but now he's become an embarrassment. Investors come here from the East and think we're uncivilized barbarians when they meet Rawlins. It's a shame, what's happened to that man."

Mrs. Akerson clucked her tongue. "Drink will do it every time. Is Captain Stone a drinking man?"

"He's not a teetotaler," Randlett replied. "I've seen him take a drink, but he doesn't stink of whiskey like Rawlins."

Clyde Akerson shook his head. "Rawlins is a disgrace, and it's not just his drinking either. It's his manners too. Most of the people in this town are afraid of him. He's a bully, pushing people around, insulting citizens who pay taxes."

Mrs. Akerson turned to Mayor Randlett. "Why don't you fire him?"

"Because we don't have anybody to replace him with."

Jennifer smiled at her father. "What about Captain Stone?"

"Captain Stone said he only intends to stay for a month."

"Maybe you can convince him to stay longer," Jennifer said. "Why don't you give him a raise? You always say that every man has his price."

"This man's price isn't dollars and cents. He seems to be motivated by something else."

"The girl," said Clyde Akerson, readjusting the napkin jammed into his collar.

"What girl?" asked Jennifer.

Her father responded, "He carries a picture of a girl with him. He's looking for her. They were supposed to get married, and she disappeared."

"How did she disappear?"

"Captain Stone came home after the war and she was gone. Neighbors told him she went west, so he's roaming the frontier looking for her."

"He's got an awful lot of ground to cover. What did she look like?"

"Pretty girl." Mayor Randlett looked at Clyde Akerson. "You saw the picture, didn't you?"

"I thought she was pretty," Randlett said. "Of course, it's hard to tell from a photograph."

The black maid, wearing a gray dress and white apron, cleared away the soup dishes. Jennifer leaned back in her chair, crossed her legs, and thought about John Stone. She didn't want anybody to know she was unduly interested in him, but she was. He'd made a favorable impression on her when she'd met him earlier in the day in her father's office. She liked his soldierly bearing and good manners, and he was handsome in a rough sort of way, but most of all she liked his smile. It was charming and warm, and he had nice teeth. She'd also liked his South Carolina drawl, his self-assurance, the ease with which he moved his tall body around.

In her opinion, she didn't have much to choose from among the men in Petie. Cowboys were crude and dirty, and their main interest seemed to be getting drunk as quickly as possible. None of the clerks and office workers interested her; they were all afraid of her father. The sons of local ranchers were a decent bunch, but there was nothing really special about them. She always figured she'd probably wind up marrying one of them someday, because a girl had to get married; she didn't want to become a spinster.

Jennifer knew she was pretty. People had been telling her that all her life. She was aware of the way men looked at her, although she didn't let on that she knew. Some men became inordinately shy in her presence, others became befuddled, and a few looked her right in the eye and left no doubts about what they wanted.

John Stone hadn't been shy or befuddled in her presence, and he hadn't given her one of those suggestive looks. He'd been calm and polite, rather self-effacing in fact, but something about him suggested tremendous power. Jennifer couldn't help feeling drawn to him, and wanted to get to know him better. There was something very interesting about him.

The maid, whose name was Esmeralda, brought a platter of roast beef to the table. Mayor Randlett stood, picked up the carving knife, and cut into the fragrant haunch of meat.

"I imagine there'll be some friction between Captain Stone and Sheriff Rawlins before long," he said. "Be interesting to see what happens."

Jennifer looked at her father. "You don't think they might actually *shoot* at each other, do you, Daddy? Don't you think somebody should warn Captain Stone?"

"I'm sure he knows which way the wind is blowing from. Captain Stone's no fool."

Clyde Akerson smiled, candlelight gleaming on his gold tooth. "It'd be nice if Sheriff Rawlins took the hint and moved on to another town that could make better use of his peculiar talents."

"Like staying drunk all day long," observed Mrs. Akerson, her eyebrows arched.

"Sheriff Rawlins is a proud man," Mayor Randlett said, laying a thick slab of roast beef on the side of the platter. "He won't give up easily."

The sign in the window said: BEST FRIED STEAKS IN TOWN.

Stone stopped and looked through the window. He was standing in front of the Acme Saloon, and it was jam-packed. He thought he'd go in and try one of those fried steaks. It'd probably be faster than waiting to be served at the Diamond Restaurant, and he should patronize as many business establishments in Petie as possible, so it wouldn't appear that he was showing favoritism.

He pushed open the swinging doors and stepped to the side,

looking the place over. The bar was to the left, the chop counter to the right, and in between were tables where men drank and gambled. Tobacco smoke was thick in the air, and waitresses carried trays of drink and food around.

A few people near the door noticed Stone, then went back to what they were doing. He made his way across the crowded floor and came to a stop at the chop counter.

A man in a dirty white jacket was behind the counter, cooking steaks in frying pans on top of a stove. Other frying pans contained sliced potatoes and onions sizzling in lard.

"What's yours?" the cook asked Stone.

"Steak and potatoes," Stone replied.

The cook speared a thick steak with a long fork and dropped it onto a plate. Then he scooped up some potatoes and onions with a spoon and flung them next to the steak. He placed the meal in front of Stone, reached under the counter for a knife and fork, slammed them down beside the plate.

Stone paid him and sliced into the steak, standing in the row with other men chewing and swallowing noisily. They had glasses of whiskey or mugs of beer beside them; the usual method was to go to the bar first, get a drink, and then carry it to the chop counter.

Stone stopped a waitress rushing by. "Get me a glass of whiskey, will you?"

Stone placed a chunk of steak into his mouth. While he was chewing, Chopak and Ramsay entered the Acme Saloon. They spotted his broad back almost instantly. Chopak chewed the end of the matchstick in his mouth and wondered if he could walk over there casually and drill Stone in the back. It appeared that he could pull it off without any trouble. It'd be all over before anybody knew what happened.

"I'll take care of the son of a bitch myself," he said to Ramsay. "You stay here and cover me."

Ramsay opened his mouth to protest, but Chopak was already in motion, twisting sideways and passing between two tables. He turned to his left and slipped between two more tables, his huge girth brushing against the backs of card players, one of whom turned around and gave him a dirty look.

Chopak moved closer to Stone, and Ramsay watched his progress from beside the door. Ramsay licked his lips nervously, because he knew all hell would break loose in a few minutes. He didn't like what Chopak was doing, but it was too late to stop him now.

Only one row of tables was between Chopak and Stone. Chopak sucked in his gut and moved between two of them, scraping against the backs of men playing cards.

"Why don't you watch where you're goin'?" one of them said.

Chopak ignored him. He was within range of John Stone now, and there was nothing to do except yank out his Colt and put a bullet in his back. He didn't see how he could miss; it was almost too easy. He lowered his hand toward his gun.

Somebody hollered out on the street: "Where's the sheriff!"

Stone spun around, and the first thing he saw was a big husky man in back of him, his legs spread apart, tensed up.

"The sheriff's in here!" shouted somebody nearby.

The big man turned away and headed toward the bar, and Stone recognized him as one of the two who'd been sitting on the bench across the street from the sheriff's office. It was a curious coincidence, or was it something else?

"Help—sheriff!" bellowed the voice outside.

Stone wiped his mouth with the back of his hand and headed toward the swinging doors. Before he reached them, a short slim man wearing a tight suit and a ruffled shirt pushed them open and burst into the Acme Saloon, looking around frantically. Stone walked toward him, and the man saw the badge on Stone's shirt.

The man's eyes were wide with excitement. "There's trouble at Miss Elsie's place! A feller with a gun is shootin' the place up!"

"Where's Miss Elsie's place?" Stone asked calmly.

"Foller me!"

The short, slim man turned around and headed back toward the door, and Stone went after him. They stepped outside and turned to the right. The man walked swiftly on his short legs, and Stone loped along easily at his side. Stone could smell the man's strong cologne.

"Anybody hurt that you know of?" Stone asked.

"I think he beat up one of the girls."

"Who're you?"

"Lester Duboff's my name. I work at Miss Elsie's place."

A gunshot rang out in the distance, then another.

"That's him," said Duboff. "Jesus, I hope he ain't killed nobody."

They moved side by side down the street, passing darkened storefronts, and turned the corner near the Olympia Hotel. A crowd was gathered in front of a three-story building farther down the block. As Stone drew closer, he saw women with painted faces, some wearing fancy dresses and others in their robes, and the men were in varying stages of undress.

They watched Stone approach. A middle-aged woman with a large bust and curly blond hair, working a fan nervously, detached herself from the crowd and advanced toward Stone. She wore a low-cut purple gown and had a large beauty mark on the top of her left breast, quivering with every step she took.

Duboff rushed forward and got between Stone and the woman. "This is Miss Elsie Moran," he said to Stone, bowing slightly, making the introduction.

"What's the problem?" Stone asked.

"A customer is shooting up my establishment," she said. "Where's Rawlins?"

"I'm on duty tonight. My name's John Stone. Anybody hurt up there?"

"I think he beat up one of my girls. She sure was screaming loud enough to be getting beat up, but I didn't see it with my own eyes."

"Where's she now?"

"Up there with him."

"Anybody else in the building?"

"He's got one of the other girls with him too."

"Where is he exactly?"

"Somewhere on the top floor."

"Get all your people away from here."

Miss Elsie had a robust voice, and she ordered everybody to move toward the hotel down the street. Stone looked up at the building and saw a red lamp on either side of the door. Bright light glowed through many of the windows on all three floors. Two shots were fired in rapid succession somewhere in the building, followed by screams of women muffled by the walls of the building.

Stone clicked his teeth. The only thing to do was go in and locate the drunk with the gun, and the drunk would probably see Stone before Stone saw him. It was a bad situation, and it was only his first night on the job.

Miss Elsie walked up to him. "Maybe you should get Sheriff Rawlins to help you."

"I'd appreciate it if you'd accompany your people down the street, ma'am."

Miss Elsie fanned herself briskly as she followed the crowd shuffling down the street toward the hotel. She and they looked back over their shoulders at Stone, who pulled the Colt out of his right holster.

There was only one thing to do. He had to go into the building and somehow disarm the drunk with the gun. He squared his shoulders and walked toward the front steps, climbing them and crossing the wide veranda. Opening the front door of the building, he looked inside, his pistol cocked, pointing straight ahead. He saw a large crystal chandelier in the middle of the ceiling, hovering over plush furniture covered with a shiny maroon fabric and trimmed with gold ruffles. The wallpaper was pale blue, and the fragrance of perfume was heavy in the air.

Another shot was fired on one of the upper floors. Stone moved quickly over the thick rug to the staircase and went up it two stairs at a time, looking to the next floor, ready to shoot at anything that moved. He heard a slapping sound and the shriek of a woman coming from one of the upper floors.

He reached the second floor and moved to the flight of stairs that led to the top floor.

"You goddamn bitch!" shouted a masculine voice above him. "I'll goddamn kill you, you talk back to me!"

"I ain't talkin' back to you!" a woman whimpered.

Stone heard the slapping sound again, followed by the scream of the woman. Then the gun fired. Stone climbed the stairs silently, keeping his back close to the wall, pointing the gun up toward the third floor.

"I think I'm gonna kill you anyways!" the man said. "I'm gonna gutshot you and watch you die real slow!"

The woman screamed hysterically, and Stone came to the third floor. It was like the landing below, a hallway lined with doors. Some of the doors were open and some closed. Articles of men's and women's clothing lay on the floor, left by those who'd departed hastily.

Stone pressed his back against the wall and took a deep breath. The woman screamed again, and it sounded as if she was toward the end of the hallway, but Stone couldn't be sure of which room she was in.

"I'll teach you to go through my pockets, you rotten little whore!"

Stone advanced noiselessly down the hallway. The woman screeched again, and he thought the sound came from the next to last room on the hallway.

He stopped beside the door to the room, his finger tightening around the trigger of his pistol. He pressed his ear to the door, and heard the squeaking of a bedspring on the other side.

"How does that feel, you bitch!" the man said.

The woman didn't reply, and Stone thought he'd better act quickly. He moved in front of the door and took two steps backward. Then he rushed the door, angling his left shoulder toward it. He reached for the doorknob, twisted, and the door was locked. Then his shoulder, with the full weight of his body behind it, struck the door, which burst open, and Stone exploded into the room.

A naked brunette woman was on her knees, tied to a bedpost, and a man wearing only jeans stood over her, strangling her with one of her undergarments. The man had black hair that hung over his eyes, and a thick mat of black hair on his chest. He looked up at Stone and froze in amazement.

Stone pointed his pistol at him. "Hold it right there!" he said.

The man snarled like a wild animal and jumped at Stone, who dodged to the side and smashed the man over the head with his pistol as the man went flying by. The man gurgled and fell to the floor, where he lay still, blood welling out of the gash on his head.

The woman tied to the bedpost was unconscious, her face pale blue, blood on her nose and mouth. Stone unwrapped the petticoat from around her neck and loosened the torn bedclothes that bound her hands. He lifted her gently and lay her on the mussed bed; her body was covered with bruises. Then he moved toward the closet. He turned the doorknob and it was locked, but a key stuck out of the hole. He twisted the key and tried the door again.

It opened, and he saw a semiclad blond woman kneeling on the floor, looking at him with terror in her eyes. He grasped her hand and pulled her up. She had a black eye and a bruise on her shoulder, but otherwise seemed okay. She raised her fists to her face and screamed, "Watch out!"

Stone spun around and saw the man on his knees, blood dripping down the side of his face, and reaching for the gun in a holster hanging from the back of a chair.

"Hold it right there!" Stone said, his hand streaking down to his Colt.

"You son of a bitch!" the man hollered, and he yanked the gun out of his holster.

Stone fired, and the room thundered with the sound of the shot. Blood gushed out of the man's stomach, and almost simultaneously his gun went off, but it was pointed down and to the side, and his bullet blew a hole in the wall beside the dresser.

The blonde shrieked, diving to the floor, and the man was on his knees, looking at Stone with glassy eyes. Blood trickled out of the corner of his mouth as he tried to bring his gun around for another shot at Stone, and Stone fired again, hitting the man in the heart. He cried out, dropped the gun, and pitched forward onto his face.

The room was full of gunsmoke. Stone stepped forward and picked up the man's gun, jamming it into his belt. He dropped to one knee and turned the man over onto his back. The man was limp and covered with blood. Stone felt his pulse. There was nothing.

"What happened?" Stone asked.

The blonde raised herself from the floor and pulled her hair back from her eyes. "I was in the next room with a customer, and I heard a commotion in this room. I came over here and knocked on the door to see what was goin' on, which was a mistake, I guess, because he grabbed me and started beatin' on me, and then he throwed me in the closet and locked the door. I heard him beatin' on Dottie but I couldn't do nothin' about it. It was awful."

She tied the belt of her robe and walked barefoot to the bed, gazing at Dottie, whose chest rose and fell with her breathing, her eyes closed. Stone dropped his Colt in its holster and looked at the man lying on the floor in an ever-widening pool of blood.

"She's comin' around," said the blonde.

Stone turned and advanced toward the bed. Dottie's eyes were half opened, and the blonde held her hand.

Dottie's throat was discolored where the man had tried to strangle her, and her naked body was gawky and pale.

"Stay with her," Stone said to the blonde. "I'll get a doctor."

"You're not gonna leave me here with *him*, are you?"

"He's dead."

"I don't care what he is. I don't want to be in the same room as him."

Stone grabbed the dead man by his pant leg and dragged him out of the room, leaving a trail of blood behind him. He pulled him across the hallway and down the stairs to the main living room, then out to the veranda of the building, letting him go. The body lay sprawled on the veranda as Stone descended the steps to the street and walked back toward the center of town.

The crowd moved up the street toward him, and Miss Elsie Moran was in front, with Lester Duboff at her side.

"What happened?" she asked.

"He's dead, and Dottie's not in very good condition. Where can I find a doctor?"

Miss Elsie turned to Duboff. "Get Dr. McGrath!"

Duboff ran back to town. The crowd circled around Stone, looking up at him.

"How's Mae?" asked Miss Elsie.

"She's taking care of Dottie. Maybe you'd better go back and help her."

Stone pushed through the crowd, which had grown considerably larger as citizens from all over the town were drawn to the excitement. The onlookers moved aside to let Stone pass, gazing at him in silence and morbid fascination.

He returned to the center of town, entering the sheriff's office. Lighting the lamp, he rolled a cigarette and sat at

Pritchard's desk, inhaling the strong smoke. His hands were steady and he felt calm; it wasn't the first time he'd killed somebody.

Something was bothering him, and he couldn't remember exactly what it was. He still was a little off balance from what had happened at Miss Elsie's place. It was like a song with a wrong note in it, or a puzzle with a piece missing.

Then he remembered the big man with the tattoo on his arm, standing behind him at the Acme Saloon. Stone had turned around and seen the man poised, staring at him with an expression of hatred on his face. Stone's first impression was that the man had been about to shoot him in the back.

Stone realized that he'd have to be more careful, and always keep his back to the wall. He'd been on the frontier long enough to know that many trigger-happy maniacs were wandering around, trying to make reputations for themselves by shooting famous gunfighters and lawmen. Before becoming deputy sheriff, Stone had been just another face in the crowd. Nobody had paid much attention to him, but now he wore a tin badge and attracted attention. He'd have to watch out for the man with the tattoo and other men with guns who might want to shoot him.

I need a drink, he thought. He poked his cigarette into the corner of his mouth and stood, blowing out the lamp. Leaving the sheriff's office, he stepped onto the boardwalk and looked around cautiously.

No one was in the immediate area. He locked the door of the sheriff's office and walked toward the Paradise Saloon, his boots clomping on the wooden planks and his spurs jangling. It occurred to him that he hadn't seen Mortimer all day. He'd have to go to the stable later and find out how he was.

Stone came to the Paradise Saloon, its light spilling into the street from its windows. Men sat out in front, and some stood on the boardwalk, talking with each other.

They looked up as Stone approached, and he searched among them quickly for the man with the tattoo on his arm, but he wasn't there. Stone pushed open the doors and entered the saloon, stepping out of the doorway into the shadows, his eyes scanning back and forth. When he was satisfied that the man with the tattoo wasn't in sight, he walked toward the bar.

People looked at him curiously; word had gotten around about the shootout at Miss Elsie's.

He stepped up to the bar and placed his foot on the brass rail. The bartender wore a dirty apron and had combed his black stringy hair over his bald spot.

"Whiskey," said Stone.

The bartender placed a glass and a bottle in front of him. Stone poured some whiskey into the glass and drank it down. Then he remembered that his back was to the door, and turned around suddenly.

Nobody was behind him, ready to draw a pistol. All he saw were the usual gamblers and drinkers. A few looked at him, and one pointed at him while murmuring to someone else. Stone rolled another cigarette and lit it, then he poured himself more whiskey. He raised the glass to his lips and let the warm amber liquid roll over his tongue and down his throat.

No wonder Rawlins is a drunk, he thought. *I'd probably be one too if I were a lawman for as long as he.*

On the prairie about three miles out of town, Mike Chopak and Fred Ramsay rode side by side, heading back to Deke Casey's outlaw camp. A full moon hung near the mountains on the horizon, and the Milky Way blazed across the sky.

"I almost had him," growled Chopak. "Another second and he would've been dead meat. If only that shit didn't break out. I couldn't've missed." Chopak grit his teeth, reliving the moment. "I almost had the son of a bitch. He was there for me."

Chopak fell silent, brooding over his lost opportunity.

"Don't take it so hard," Ramsay told him. "It was a bad break. We'll get him some other way, don't you worry about it."

"I wanted him for myself."

"You're gittin' yourself all worked up over nothin'."

"I don't like John Stone. There's something about him that pisses me off."

Chopak ground his teeth together and was itchy all over. John Stone had killed eight members of the gang and everybody in Petie treated him like God. Chopak pulled back on the reins of his horse, and the horse came to a stop.

"What's the matter?" Ramsay asked.

"I'm goin' back."

"You're crazy! He knows who you are!"

"He won't see me this time. You don't haveta come with me if you don't wanna. I'll handle him myself."

Ramsay shrugged. "I ain't gonna argue with you, Chopak. Do what you wanna. I'm goin' back to camp."

Ramsay put the spurs to his horse, which ambled forward, leaving Chopak behind. Chopak wheeled his horse around and headed back toward Petie, whose lights glowed in the distance.

A faint smile creased Chopak's bearded face. He thought of John Stone lying in the dust, a bullet in his back. "This time I'll git you," Chopak muttered. "This time you won't git away."

Stone finished his drink and placed the glass on the bar. He thought he shouldn't have another one, because he was on duty.

He leaned his back against the bar and looked at the other customers, and they were the usual bunch of cowboys on a spree, businessmen talking over deals, card sharps trying to win their pots by hook or crook, and solitary drinkers muttering to themselves, disheveled and forlorn.

The doors of the saloon were pushed open, and Sheriff Rawlins stepped inside. He wore his long black frock coat that nearly reached his knees, his black hat, and his badge on the lapel of his coat. Sheriff Rawlins stopped, looked around, and his eyes fell on Stone. He frowned, then walked to the other end of the bar. His gait was steady and sure, but his face was flushed and Stone suspected he was drunk.

"Whiskey!" Rawlins called out loudly.

Stone rolled a cigarette. He heard a bottle and a glass being placed on the end of the bar in front of Rawlins.

"I can see," Rawlins said in his deep booming voice, "that the town hero is in here tonight. Well, I feel real proud to be here. Maybe I ought to take a walk down the bar there and kiss his ass just like everybody else in this mealy-mouthed goddamn town."

The music stopped and a hush fell over the saloon. Stone scraped his match over the top of the bar and lit his cigarette. The men between Rawlins and Stone got out of the way, carrying their drinks.

Rawlins turned to the side and faced Stone, who still leaned his back against the bar.

"What's it feel like to be the town hero, Deputy?" Rawlins asked, a sarcastic tang in his voice.

Stone turned and looked at Rawlins, who stood casually with his elbow resting against the bar and one foot slightly in front of the other. A strange uneasy smile was on Rawlins's face.

"I believe I just asked you a question, Deputy," Rawlins said.

Their eyes met, and Stone saw a ruined man. Stone couldn't help feeling sorry for him, and couldn't bring himself to respond with an insult.

Instead he headed for the doors, and after a few steps it occurred to him that he was committing the worst insult of all, because he was ignoring Rawlins.

"Hey—goddamn you!" Rawlins shouted.

Stone continued to walk toward the doors. He pushed them open and stepped onto the boardwalk, leaving Rawlins alone at the bar.

Rawlins was so angry his ears had turned red. He'd expected to humiliate Stone in front of the other patrons, but Stone had just walked away and made him appear foolish. Rawlins looked around and spotted Thad Cooper, a local lawyer and member of the town council, seated at the table nearest him.

"What the hell're you laughin' at, Cooper!"

"I wasn't laughing at anything, Sheriff."

"Don't you goddamn laugh at me!"

Rawlins walked toward Cooper, grabbed him by the front of his shirt, and lifted him off the chair. Cooper went pale, and his lips quivered as Rawlins raised him into the air, bringing his face so close Cooper could smell the alcohol on his breath.

"I never liked you," Rawlins said. "I always thought you was a spineless son of a bitch. Don't you ever laugh at me again."

"I wasn't laughing at you, Sheriff."

Rawlins narrowed his eyes. "Are you callin' me a liar?"

Cooper shook his head. "No, Sheriff," he stuttered.

"You better not, because I'd kick yer ass as soon as look at you."

Sheriff Rawlins threw Cooper across the room, and Cooper

stumbled backward, landing on the table in back of him, scattering the chips and cards lying upon it, startling the gamblers. Rawlins returned to the bar, reached for his glass, and dumped its contents down his throat.

"Goddamn cheap politicians," he said. "Wouldn't know a bull's ass from a banjo."

Mike Chopak tethered his horse to a tree on the outskirts of town. He dismounted, pulled his rifle out of its boot, and ducked into the shadows.

It was silent and not a light was on in any of the buildings around him. He moved through the back alleys of Petie, skirting the edges of buildings, always staying in the darkness. If he heard a sound he froze until he was sure he could move without being observed.

He made his way toward the sheriff's office, and finally crept down the alley that led to the segment of the street where it was located. He gazed across the street to the sheriff's office and saw the darkened windows, wondering whether Stone was asleep inside or out someplace in the town.

He knew he couldn't just barge into the sheriff's office and start shooting, because he wouldn't be able to see what he was shooting at. He'd have to be smarter than that and position himself in a place where he could bushwhack Stone when Stone either came out of the office or went into it.

Where's a good place? Chopak asked himself. Obviously it was somewhere across the street. Chopak poked his head out of the alley again and looked left and right. Nobody was around. He moved onto the boardwalk and walked toward the sheriff's office, looking for possible places to hide.

He came to the building across the street from the sheriff's office, and it was a ladies dress shop closed for the night. Advancing toward the door, he turned the knob, but it was locked just as he expected. Taking his jackknife out of his pocket, he inserted it in the crack between the door and the frame, but couldn't jimmy it open.

"Shit," he muttered, closing the jackknife and dropping it into his pocket. It would've been an ideal spot for an ambush. Then he had an idea. *Maybe I can get up on the roof.* It was a two-story building, and probably had a set of stairs on the outside in back. He slunk into the alley and walked to the rear of the building.

The full moon shone overhead, and Chopak saw the stairway leading up to the second floor. He figured the people who owned the store probably lived up there, or rented it to someone else. Either way, he could assume that people were sleeping on the top floor, and he had to be silent.

He climbed the stairs on his tiptoes, holding on to the banister for support. When he reached the second floor he saw a ladder affixed to the building and extending to the roof, so the roof and chimney would be accessible for repair.

He climbed the ladder and crawled onto the roof, lifting his arms and legs high and bringing them down softly on the wood shingles, so he'd make no sound. Finally he came to the peak. Removing his hat and placing it beside him, he raised his head slowly until he could see the sheriff's office across the street.

It was a perfect view, and he congratulated himself for being so smart. Now all he had to do was make himself as comfortable as possible and wait for John Stone. *The son of a bitch is as good as dead*, he thought, bringing his rifle closer, aiming down the barrel at the front door.

The full moon illuminated the sidewalk clearly, and it would be an easy shot. *At this distance, I can't miss*, he said to himself.

Stone walked into the dark stable and smelled the strong aroma of horses. They were lined up in two rows of stalls on either side of him, and some of them shuffled their hooves as he passed by.

"Who's there?" asked a voice.

"Deputy Sheriff John Stone."

A man with a walrus mustache came out of the shadows, holding a rifle in his hands, looking at Stone suspiciously. "Lookin' for yer horse?"

"That's right."

"He's over there."

The man pointed, and Stone moved in that direction, passing horse after horse until he heard a familiar snort.

"Mortimer," Stone said.

The big black animal turned his head around and looked at

him. Stone stepped into the stall and patted his mane. Mortimer made a funny motion with his lips, and his eyes were huge and gleaming.

"I haven't forgotten you," Stone said, scratching Mortimer's neck. "I've been busy, you see. Figured you needed some rest anyway. We were on the trail together for a long time, weren't we? Maybe tomorrow or the next day we can go someplace."

Mortimer whinnied and shook his head from side to side. Stone took a step back and admired him. He was a fabulous animal, fleet as the wind, with incredible endurance. A rancher had given Mortimer to Stone, and Mortimer was said to've been the fastest horse in that county.

"Are they treating you all right?" Stone asked. "Getting enough to eat?"

Stone stood beside the horse, patting him and murmuring softly. Stone's father had owned a stable of fine horses back in South Carolina before the war, and Stone had ridden great animals during the war, but none was better than Mortimer.

"Sorry to wake you up," Stone said. "Just wanted to see how you were. I'll be back tomorrow, maybe bring you a little present. Take it easy, now."

Stone gave Mortimer one last pat and walked out of the stall, heading for the street. He turned toward the sheriff's office, planning to lie down on the cot and sleep for an hour. If he was lucky, nobody would bother him.

The town was deserted and still. The only sound came from his boots as they landed on the boardwalk, and the light of the full moon threw long ghostly shadows into the middle of the street. A few men were passed out on the bench in front of the Acme Saloon, and light glowed from the interior of the establishment. He thought he ought to go in and see what was going on, but decided not to look for trouble. He just wanted to get some rest.

He came to the Paradise Saloon. Two men were having an argument in front of it, but they were so drunk they were unintelligible. The piano was being played inside, and a man laughed raucously. The doors swung open and two men staggered out, their arms around each other's shoulders, singing off-key.

Stone continued on his way to the sheriff's office. He passed a drunk lying unconscious in the gutter, and a big gray rat scurried in front of Stone, diving under the boardwalk.

Stone's legs felt leaden, and he had a mild backache. All he wanted to do was to go to sleep. He couldn't wait to lie down on the cot and close his eyes.

On the roof across the street, Mike Chopak watched his every move. *Here he comes*, thought Chopak, raising the butt of his rifle to his shoulder. *This is it*.

Chopak closed one eye and lined up the sights of his rifle on the middle of Stone's torso. Stone stopped in front of the door to the sheriff's office and looked both ways, then reached into his pocket for the keys. Chopak pasted his sights on the middle of Stone's back and squeezed the trigger.

Stone pulled the keys out of his pocket and inserted them in the lock. The window on the door showed the reflection of the building behind him, and he saw something move on the roof. It looked like a man's head, and Stone dived to the ground.

On his way down, he heard a gunshot, and the glass above his head shattered. He pulled out both his Colts and, lying on his stomach, leveled a barrage of bullets at the man on the roof across the street. The man ducked his head, and Stone jumped to his feet, charging across the street and running into the alley.

Chopak realized he'd missed. Gritting his teeth and cursing himself, he knew he had to get out of there. He clambered down the steep slope of shingles toward the ladder.

Meanwhile, Stone was speeding through the alley, a Colt in each hand. He ran into the backyard and spun around, looking up at the roof, and saw a man with a rifle moving toward a ladder affixed to the side of the building.

Stone raised his Colts and opened fire. The loud explosions tore the night apart, and the man on the roof staggered. He dropped his rifle, clutched his stomach with both hands, and teetered from one side to the other. Stone shot him again, and the man's knees gave out. He dropped onto the roof and rolled down the shingles, toppling over the gutter and falling through the air, landing with a loud *thump* on the ground, where he lay still on his stomach.

Stone walked toward him, both his Colts ready to fire again, but the man wasn't moving. Stone dug his boot underneath him and flipped him over onto his back.

The first thing he saw was the tattoo of a skull on the man's meaty bicep. Stone looked at the man's face and recognized him as the one who'd been standing behind him in the Acme Saloon earlier in the evening. *Who is this son of a bitch?*

He bent over and searched through the man's pockets, hoping to find some identification, but all he came up with were a few coins, a jackknife, and a filthy handkerchief.

He heard footsteps behind him and turned around. A man in a nightshirt, carrying a rifle, approached him.

"What the hell's goin' on?"

"This man tried to shoot me."

Another man came from the other direction, a pistol in his hand. He was fully dressed, but hadn't had time to tuck in his shirt. A third man advanced through the alley, and he also carried a pistol in his hand.

Stone thumbed fresh cartridges into his Colts. He finished loading his guns and looked down at the man with the tattoo, wondering who he was. He couldn't recall ever seeing him before tonight. A few other people came out of buildings in the vicinity and joined the crowd forming around the body of the dead man.

"Who is he?" somebody asked.

"Don't know," replied Stone.

Stone puffed his cigarette and thought back to when he was inserting his key in the door of the sheriff's office. If it hadn't been a full moon, he might not've seen the man on the roof behind him reflected in the glass window, and he might be dead right now.

Two men came through the alley, one carrying a black bag.

"What's the problem here?"

"This man tried to shoot me."

The man with the black bag wore a suit and a long curving white mustache. "You're Captain Stone, aren't you? I've heard about you, but haven't had the opportunity to meet you yet. I'm Dr. McGrath, a member of the town council. Have you ever seen this man before?"

"No."

"I wonder why he tried to shoot you."

"So do I."

"He must've had something against you." Dr. McGrath

dropped to one knee and felt the man's pulse. "He won't ever try to shoot anybody else, that's for sure. Where were you when he tried to shoot you?"

"I was unlocking the door to the sheriff's office, and he was on the roof up there with a rifle."

"Sounds like he was laying for you. You sure you never saw him before?"

"I saw him earlier tonight, but that's all. We didn't have a run-in or anything like that."

"You must've offended him somehow, or offended somebody else who paid him to kill you. You can't think of anybody you might've offended?"

"I just arrived in town today, and haven't had time to offend anybody yet. You don't need me for anything else, do you, Doctor?"

"Not right now."

Stone pulled the dead man's pistol out of his holster and jammed it into his belt. Then he picked up the dead man's rifle and carried it through the alley and across the street to the sheriff's office. Dropping the rifle and pistol on Pritchard's desk, he sat on the cot underneath the framed portrait of Robert E. Lee.

He felt drained of energy, and still had several hours to go. Puffing his cigarette, he tried to figure out why the man with the tattoo had tried to shoot him. Who the hell was he?

Stone couldn't think of any enemies he had in Petie, except Sheriff Rawlins. Everybody in the town seemed favorably disposed toward him, except Rawlins. Why had the man with the tattoo made himself Stone's enemy?

He couldn't figure it out. Maybe the man with the tattoo just didn't like lawmen. Stone couldn't think of any other possible explanation.

He lay down and closed his eyes, but his nerves were jangled and he couldn't sleep. He'd killed two men and the night wasn't even half over.

He rolled over onto his side, but couldn't get comfortable. After several minutes it occurred to him that he wasn't going to get any sleep, and he decided he might as well try to stay awake until it was time for him to go off duty. He brought his feet around and placed them on the floor. *I could use some coffee*, he thought.

He stood and walked to the washbasin, splashing water on his face, drying it with the soiled towel. Then he put on his hat and left the sheriff's office.

He walked down Main Street to the Acme Saloon and went inside. Most of the crowd he'd seen earlier had gone home. There was one card game involving six men, and a number of solitary drunks scattered around at tables, staring into space. Several men stood at the bar, drinking alone or in groups. The piano player had gone home, and only one waitress was on duty. She was on the hefty side, with a large bosom and short brown hair, in her forties.

Stone plopped down at a table against the far wall, facing the front doors, and pushed his hat to the back of his head. He took out his tobacco and rolled another cigarette. The waitress walked toward him.

"Strong black coffee," Stone said.

She shuffled toward the bar. Stone lit his cigarette, and his mouth tasted foul. He wondered how long it'd take before he became accustomed to working at night and sleeping during the day. He thought the rest of the night should be quiet, because most of the drunks were asleep.

The waitress returned with a pot of coffee and a mug, which she placed in front of him, and he tossed a few coins onto her tray.

"Mind if I sit down?" she asked.

"Go right ahead."

She dropped onto the chair opposite him and sighed, pulling her hair back from her forehead. "So you're the new deputy. Glad to meet you, my name's Rosie. Heard you been havin' a busy night. Saw you and Rawlins in here a little earlier. You'd better watch out for him. He don't like you at all."

"You been in Petie long?" Stone asked, pouring himself a cup of coffee.

"I'm Rawlins's woman."

Stone looked at her with more than casual interest. She'd probably been pretty once, before she started gaining weight.

"Well, it's true," Stone said, "Rawlins doesn't have much use for me. Can't say why. I've never done anything to him. Don't even hardly know him."

"He looks at you and sees himself the way he used to be,"

Rosie said. "It makes him mad, but I reckon he's more mad at himself than he is at you. In the old days he used to walk around this town like he owned it, and everybody loved him, but people got short memories. They didn't mind his drinkin' and bad manners in the old days, as long as he was cleanin' up the town for them, but now that the town's cleaned up, they'd rather have somebody more presentable, somebody like *you*."

Stone sipped his coffee. "I'm leaving in a month. I've got other things that I want to do."

She looked askance at him. "Wait'll the mayor and the town fathers git to workin' on you. They'll offer you the moon, and you'll snap it right up."

"No, I've got things to do."

"They'll change yer mind. The big boys in this town always git what they want."

The sound of an angry voice filled the saloon. "Who in the hell do you think you're callin' a liar!"

"You, you son of a goddamn whore!"

Stone looked toward the bar and saw two men facing each other. They were dressed like cowboys and looked like they were ready to get down to it.

"Clem, you'd better apologize right here and goddamn now!" said the man on the left, who wore a plaid shirt and a hat with a torn brim.

"Like hell I will!" replied the man on the right, who was tall and lanky, with a nose like a finger.

"You no-good varmint—I'll kill you!"

The man in the plaid shirt dived on the lanky one, and they tussled in front of the bar. One of their elbows knocked over a mug of beer, and it spilled onto the floor. Men sitting at nearby tables got up and stepped backward out of the way.

Stone placed his cigarette in the ashtray. Under normal circumstances, he would've watched the fight but steered clear of it. Now he was a deputy sheriff, and had to stop it.

"Be right back," he said to Rosie.

Stone placed his hat on the table and walked toward the two men shoving each other in front of the bar.

"I always knowed you was no fuckin' good!" shouted the man in the plaid shirt.

"Go shit in yer hat and pull it down over yer ears!"

Stone approached the two men and stopped a few feet away from them. "I think you two'd better settle down," he said.

They turned and looked at him.

"Who the hell are you?" asked the one in the plaid shirt.

"Deputy Sheriff Stone. Why don't you boys go home and sleep it off?"

The man in the plaid shirt narrowed his eyes as he looked at Stone's tin badge. "Well, well, well," he said. "Look what we got here. A fuckin' *lawman*."

"Hit the trail, lawman," said the lanky man, "or else we'll take yer gun and shove it up yer ass."

"Look, Clem," said the man in the plaid shirt, "he's wearin' *two* guns."

"Oh, he must be a helluva lawman, if he's wearin' two guns. We'd better go home like he says."

The man in the plaid shirt faced Stone. "You think you're tough enough to make me go home, lawman?"

"Like I said, I think you boys'd better sleep it off."

"You gonna make me?"

"If I have to."

The man in the plaid shirt stepped forward belligerently. "You have to."

Stone smiled and held up his hands. "Let's calm down, gents. C'mon, I'll buy the both of you a drink."

"You can't buy me off," said the man in the plaid shirt. "I don't like cheap lawmen who talk big but can't back it up. You said you're gonna make me go home? Well go ahead, make me go home."

Stone looked at both of them. They were facing him, spoiling for trouble, ready to jump. He took a step backward. "Just settle down," he said, "and everything will be all right."

"It's too late for that, lawman. You done put yer nose where it don't belong. Now I'm gonna have to break it off and push it down yer throat."

"Here I stand," Stone said.

The man in the plaid shirt looked at his lanky friend and grinned, and his lanky friend grinned back. They took off their hats and laid them on the bar, then turned toward Stone and charged.

Stone picked up the chair nearest to him and crashed it over the head of the lanky man, then threw a sharp left jab into the face of the man in the plaid shirt. The man in the plaid shirt went flying back into the bar, bounced off it, and came at Stone again, hurtling a punch toward Stone's jaw, but Stone timed him coming in, dodged the punch, and landed a powerful right cross to the point of his jaw. The impact of the blow raised the man a few inches off the floor and sent him sprawling backward against the bar again.

Meanwhile, the lanky man raised himself groggily from the floor and touched his hand to his scalp. His fingers came back with blood on them, and he let out a roar of displeasure as he dived toward Stone, tackling him and knocking him backward.

Stone fell onto a table covered with cards, poker chips, and glasses, and the table collapsed. The lanky cowboy landed on Stone and raised his fist, trying to punch Stone in the mouth, but Stone caught his fist in his left hand and grabbed the lanky cowboy's throat with his right hand. He squeezed with all his strength, and the lanky man gagged, his face turning blue. Stone hurled him away and climbed to his feet just as the man in the plaid shirt jumped on him again.

Stone fell back onto the floor, and the man in the plaid shirt was on top of him in an instant. He slammed his fist into Stone's mouth, but Stone always had been able to take a good punch. The cowboy raised his fist to punch again, but Stone hit him first with a rocking blow to the left eye, and the cowboy lost his balance. Stone pushed him away and got to his feet just as the lanky man dived on him, knocking him to the floor again.

This time Stone rolled when he hit the floor and jumped to his feet quickly, raising his fists. His two adversaries attacked him from both sides, and he took a step back to get some punching room. They converged on him, hurling blows at his head, and he ducked underneath their fists, shooting a powerful jab into the gut of the man in the plaid shirt, who was on Stone's left, and then Stone sidestepped farther to the left to get out of the range of the lanky man's punches.

The man in the plaid shirt was bent over with the worst stomachache of his life, and Stone brought both his fists down on his head, propelling him toward the floor, which the man struck with his face, flattening his nose and knocking himself unconscious.

The lanky man jumped over his fallen friend and reached his fingers toward Stone's throat, but Stone whacked the man's arms out of the way with his left hand and hooked him between the eyes with his right hand. The lanky man stopped cold, stunned momentarily, so Stone hooked him again with his right hand, jabbed him with his left, and smashed him in the face with his right. The lanky man stumbled backward and fell onto a table. Stone lifted him by his shirt and threw him into the air. The lanky man flew over the bar and crashed against the rows of bottles on the shelves behind the bar, then dropped unconscious to the floor.

"Watch out!" somebody shouted.

Stone turned around and saw the man in the plaid shirt standing there with his face a bloody mask and a bottle in his hands.

"I'm gonna cut yer fuckin' throat," the man said, breaking the bottle on the table beside him.

Whiskey and shards of glass splattered in all directions, and the jagged edge of the bottle glinted in the light of the lamps as the man in the plaid shirt held it up in the air.

"Are you sure that's the way you want it?" Stone asked.

"That's the way I want it."

Stone reached into his boot and pulled out his knife. "Are you still sure that's the way you want it?"

The man in the plaid shirt bellowed like a wild animal and rushed toward Stone, pushing the broken bottle toward Stone's throat. Stone dodged to the side and jammed the blade of his knife into the man's wrist, and the man's forward motion caused the blade to rip his arm open nearly all the way to his shoulder. The man closed his eyes and screamed horribly as blood spurted out of the arteries in his arm. He dropped the bottle involuntarily, and Stone stepped forward, putting all of his weight behind a left hook. It landed on the man's forehead, and his knees sagged. Stone hit him again, this time in the mouth, and the man stumbled backward, falling against the bar, striking his head against it, and dropping sideways to the floor.

The lanky man raised his head behind the bar, displaying a black eye, a split lip, and a dazed expression.

"Want some more?" Stone asked.

The lanky man looked at the bloody knife in Stone's hand and shook his head. Stone wiped the knife on the pant leg of the man lying on the floor, and thrust the knife back into his boot.

"Call the doctor," he said to the bartender.

He walked across the saloon to the table where he'd been sitting and dropped onto the chair, reaching for his cup of coffee. He raised the cup to his lips and drained it dry.

Rosie stood beside the table. "Can I get you anything else?" she asked.

"Whiskey," he said.

Rosie walked toward the bar. Stone lifted his cigarette out of the ashtray and took a drag. *The shit a person has to go through to earn a living.* He looked at the man lying in a widening pool of blood in front of the bar. His lanky friend tried to bandage his arm with a length of torn shirt. Stone wondered whether he should arrest both of them. He supposed they'd been disturbing the peace, and he believed it was illegal in most places to attack an officer of the law. *Guess I'll have to arrest them.*

Rosie returned with a bottle of whiskey and a glass. "That was some fight."

Stone poured himself three fingers of whiskey and drank it down. Wiping his mouth with the back of his hand, he stood and put on his hat. He walked toward the lanky man, who was tying the bandage around his friend's arm.

"You and he are under arrest," Stone said. Reaching down, he pulled the gun out of the lanky man's holster. "Get moving."

"What about my pardner?"

"I'll take care of him. Get moving, and if you start up with me again, I'll kill you."

The lanky man scowled as he walked toward the door. Stone grabbed the collar of the other man and dragged him away from the bar, leaving a trail of blood behind him.

"When the doctor comes," Stone said to the bartender, "tell him his patient's in jail."

Stone dragged the man in the plaid shirt out of the bar and onto the sidewalk. The lanky man, who was walking ahead, turned around to look.

"Keep going," Stone told him. "The jail's straight ahead."

"My pardner's gonna bleed to death."

"He shouldn't go at people with broken bottles."

Stone made his way toward his office, pulling the unconscious man in the plaid shirt behind him. Stone's mouth hurt from where he'd been punched during the fight, and he had a cut on his forehead. *I don't think I'll last a month if every night's gonna be like this*, he thought.

Tom Hurley lurked behind the boulder, holding his rifle in his hands, aiming at the rider approaching along the moonlit trail. The rider came closer and Hurley squinted his eyes at him. If he was a stranger, Hurley'd shoot him dead, but it was unlikely that a stranger would wander into Deke Casey's outlaw camp in the middle of the night.

"It's me!" called Fred Ramsay. "Put the goddamned rifle down."

Hurley lowered the rifle and stepped out from behind the boulder. "Where's Chopak?"

"In town."

"How come?"

"He's gone loco, I think."

Ramsay rode up the winding trail to the campsite, where men slept around the charred remains of a fire. They stirred as Ramsay approached, and when they saw who it was, they sat up and wrapped their blankets around them.

Ramsay picketed his horse and pulled off the saddle. He hoisted the saddle onto his shoulders and carried it toward the circle of outlaws, dropping it to the ground.

Moonlight shone on the gathering of men, and they were unshaven and dirty, their gunbelts close by. Casey lit his cigarette with a match and blew smoke out of his nose.

"Why'd Chopak stay in town?" he asked.

"He wanted to shoot John Stone. That's the galoot who killed our men."

"Why didn't you stay with him?"

"I thought you told us to come back and tell you what was goin' on. You said not to start any shit ourselves."

"You should've stuck with Chopak."

"I'm damned if I do, and damned if I don't."

"You see Stone?"

"Yeah, I seen him. Big feller, carries two Colts. They made him deputy sheriff. Chopak tried to back-shoot him in a bar, but Stone saw him first and it didn't work. Chopak and me left town, but then Chopak turned around and went back, so's he could bushwhack Stone. Maybe Stone's dead by now, I don't know. Stone got a good look at Chopak, so Chopak'll have to be careful. Stone ain't nobody to fuck with."

Casey puffed his cigarette in silence, trying not to get mad. The men often disobeyed orders, and he didn't like it. It was hard to control them.

"You find out where Stone lives?" he asked Ramsay.

"At the hotel. He works nights out of the sheriff's office."

Casey knew where the hotel and the sheriff's office were. He'd studied the town in detail when he'd planned the bank robbery. It had been like a military operation and would've worked if it hadn't been for John Stone.

He knew where Stone lived and worked, so it wouldn't be difficult to track him down. There were six men left in the gang, and that should be plenty.

Casey inhaled his cigarette and blew smoke into the air. "Tomorrow night we'll shoot John Stone," he said.

"What if Chopak already got him?" asked Ramsay.

"If Chopak already got him, then we can't git him twice. But if Chopak didn't get him, then we'll find him and shoot him down like a dog. Then we'll tie him up behind one of our horses and drag his body through town. We'll show them people what kind of hero he is, and then we'll hit that bank again, only this time we'll take every goddamn penny out of it." He held the cigarette between his fingers, and its tip glowed cherry red in the darkness. "Nobody messes with the Deke Casey gang and gets away with it," he said. "John Stone has got to die."

4

IT WAS MORNING in Petie, and the sun shone brightly in the sky. Dr. McGrath carried his little black bag along the sidewalk and stopped in front of Mayor Randlett's law office, opened the door, and went inside.

Jennifer sat behind the front desk, and her father was pulling papers out of a file cabinet.

"Morning," said Dr. McGrath sleepily.

"You look like hell, Bill," Mayor Randlett said. "What happened?"

"Been up all night. Two shootings and one knifing. Every time I went to bed, somebody woke me up and I had to go out again. Think I'm gonna take today off and try to catch up on my sleep."

"How'd our new deputy sheriff hold up?"

"Somebody tried to bushwhack him from the roof opposite the sheriff's office. Don't know who it was. Before that he had to shoot a drunken cowboy at Miss Elsie's. Then there was a knife and bottle fracas at the Acme. He had a bad night. Also heard he had a run-in with Rawlins. Seems Rawlins cursed him out at the Paradise in front of a lot of people, but Stone ignored him and nothing came of it. Hope Stone isn't getting discouraged with the job too quick. He's a good man and I'd hate to see us lose him."

"I'll have a talk with him," Randlett replied. "Most nights around here are pretty quiet."

"Two men are in jail. One of them's hurt pretty bad. He went at Stone with a broken bottle, and Stone nearly cut his arm off with that knife he carries."

"Stone's a tough customer. No doubt about it. He's just what this town needs."

"Thought I'd drop by to let you know what happened last night. Know you like to stay on top of things."

Dr. McGrath left Randlett's office, and Jennifer said to her father, "Why don't you invite John Stone to dinner tonight? Then you could talk with him in a comfortable setting, and he'd be more receptive to what you had to say."

Mayor Randlett thought about it for a few moments. "Good idea. I'll ask him later today."

A huge wagon filled with crates rolled past the Olympia Hotel, and the freighter flicked his whip at the haunch of one of his horses. "Move on there, you son of a bitch!" he hollered at the top of his lungs.

John Stone opened his eyes. It was the third time he'd been awakened that morning. His window faced the street, and the noise was constant. He rolled out of bed and rubbed his eyes.

Curtains covered the window, but the bright morning sun peeked through anyway. He had a headache and felt sick to his stomach. Two men were talking on the sidewalk in front of the hotel, and he could hear practically every word. He couldn't close his window, because the room'd get too hot.

The only thing to do was change his room. He got up, dressed, and descended the stairs to the lobby.

"What can I do for you, Deputy?" asked the desk clerk, Howard Conway.

"My room's too noisy, and I was wondering if you might have something quiet at the back of the hotel."

"We're all full up today. Sorry. Maybe we can find something for you tomorrow."

Stone climbed the stairs and returned to his room. He undressed, dropped into bed, and covered his head with the pillow. Outside on the street three cowboys galloped by on their horses, and their horses' hooves sounded as if they were pounding inside Stone's brain.

A promise is a promise, Stone thought, *but if I don't find someplace quiet to sleep pretty soon, I might have to leave this town early.*

Thad Cooper walked into Mayor Randlett's office. "I'd like to speak with your father," he said to Jennifer.

"Anything wrong?"

"Sheriff Rawlins again."

At that moment the door to the back office opened, and Mayor Randlett rushed out, carrying a sheaf of legal documents in his hand. "Morning, Thad," Mayor Randlett said. "You say something about our sheriff?"

"I had a run-in with him last night at the Acme. He attacked me for no reason at all, insulted me, and slapped me in front of the crowd there. It was quite humiliating, and there was nothing I could do about it. I and a lot of other people are getting pretty fed up with the antics of Rawlins. The man's completely out of hand. I *am* a member of the town council, after all. If he thinks he can slap me around, what's he going to do with the ordinary citizens of this town? I think we ought to consider having a special meeting of the council to discuss getting rid of Rawlins for once and for all. I think when he starts pushing around elected public officials, he's going too far."

"We can fire him, Thad. That's no problem. But we don't have anybody to replace him with yet, and we need a sheriff. Whether you like Rawlins or not, you've got to admit that he keeps the lid on this town."

"What about our new deputy?"

"That's a possibility that we're working on, but we don't have him yet. It might take some doing to convince him to accept the job. He said he's leaving after a month."

"Offer him more money."

"I think I'd better have a talk with Rawlins first. He's done a lot for this town. We have to give him a chance."

"He's had all the chances he should get. He's a drunk and a bully, and I don't think we should put up with him anymore.

We'd be better off with a volunteer vigilante group than with Rawlins."

Mayor Randlett gazed into Cooper's eyes. "Who's going to be in the volunteer vigilante group?"

"I'm sure somebody'd join."

"You?"

"Well, I'm kind of busy."

"So's everybody else. The plain fact is that nobody wants to put his life on the line. That's why we need Rawlins. We're stuck with him until we can find somebody else. But I'll talk with him. Maybe he'll listen to reason."

Sheriff Rawlins approached the front door of his office and noticed that the window was shattered. He opened the door and stepped inside.

"What the hell happened to the window?" he asked Pritchard.

"Somebody tried to bushwhack Deputy Stone from the roof across the street, but Stone shot him first."

Sheriff Rawlins was puzzled by the news. Why should anybody want to bushwhack Stone?

"Was Stone hurt?" Rawlins asked.

"Not a scratch."

Rawlins moved toward his desk, his eyes bloodshot and his gait unsteady. His hands shook slightly as he took off his hat and hung it on the peg.

"Anything else happen last night?"

Pritchard picked up a sheet of paper from his desk. "Deputy Stone shot a cowboy who was trying to strangle Miss Dorothy Brenner over at Miss Elsie's. Then he arrested two cowboys at the Paradise. Seems they attacked him and he cut one of them pretty bad with a knife."

"Why the knife?"

"The feller attacked him with a broken bottle."

Rawlins unlocked the door to the jail area and walked back to the cells. In the dim light, he saw two men. One lay on a cot, his arm bandaged, unconscious, his skin pale and face bruised. The other was awake, but his nose was bandaged. He looked like he'd been in a war.

"I think I got a broken rib," the man with the bandaged nose said. "Every time I move it hurts."

"Tell it to the judge," Rawlins replied.

Rawlins left the jail area and sat at his desk. He opened the bottom drawer, took out his bottle, and raised it to his lips. His hands stopped shaking after a few swallows.

He put a stogie into his mouth and lit it up. Who'd want to bushwhack John Stone? It was nagging his mind, because it didn't make sense. Stone had just arrived in town, and hadn't been here long enough to make enemies. Maybe the bushwhacker was somebody from his past who'd finally caught up with him. Sheriff Rawlins thought Stone might be a wanted man himself. He decided to look over the wanted posters to see if he could pick him out.

The door opened as Rawlins was about to get the stack of wanted posters. He looked up and saw Mayor Randlett enter the office. Rawlins realized he hadn't put the bottle of whiskey away, and that didn't look so good.

Mayor Randlett wore a derby hat, which he didn't bother to take off, and he didn't appear very happy.

"What's this about you insulting Thad Cooper and pushing him around at the Acme last night?" Mayor Randlett demanded.

Sheriff Rawlins stared at him in amazement, because he didn't remember insulting Thad Cooper and pushing him around at the Acme. Rawlins often had blackouts due to his heavy drinking. He recalled having a run-in with Stone, but couldn't remember anything about Thad Cooper.

Rawlins looked up at Mayor Randlett and scowled. "What about it!"

"We're getting sick and tired of you pushing around the citizens of this town."

"Maybe they need to get pushed around."

"Thad is a respected citizen and a member of the town council. You seem to forget, Sheriff Rawlins, that you're working for us, and we're not working for you. We're paying you to enforce law and order in this town, not bully the citizens. We've warned you before, and we're coming to the end of our rope with you. We need a sheriff, but your belligerent behavior is becoming more of a problem than we can bear. Nobody's indispensable, Sheriff Rawlins. I must ask you to bear that in mind in the future."

Rawlins spat into the brass cuspidor near his desk. Then he raised his whiskey bottle and took a swig, to antagonize Mayor Randlett further. He rinsed his mouth with the fiery whiskey, then swallowed it down.

"You're talkin' pretty big, now that you got a new deputy. I reckon you're aimin' to move him into my job first thing you get, is that right, Randlett?"

"We have no plans along those lines."

"You can't fool me, but let me tell you somethin'. John Stone ain't what you think he is. I believe he's a wanted man."

Mayor Randlett blinked in surprise. "What makes you say that?"

"I ain't been a lawman for twenty years without learnin' somethin'. I know you damn people around here think I'm dumb, but I ain't. You're gonna have shit on your face when word gets around that you hired a wanted man to be deputy."

"Sheriff Rawlins, when you have proof of what you say, present it to me. Until then, I don't want to hear it."

"You're like everybody else in this damn town. You don't want to know the truth."

"It's not the truth until you show me the wanted poster with John Stone's face on it."

Sheriff Rawlins puffed his stogie and wondered if he'd gone too far. He had no proof that John Stone was a wanted man, but somehow the words had blurted out of his mouth.

"I got work to do," Sheriff Rawlins said. "If you don't mind."

"I'm not finished yet," Mayor Randlett replied. "I want you to understand this: If we have any more trouble with you, we'll have to take it up at the next meeting of the town council."

"What's that supposed to mean?"

"Just what you think it means."

"Without me, you'll have outlaws, thieves, and crooks thick as locusts in this town. You've never appreciated what I've done for you."

"We appreciate what you've done for us, but we don't appreciate what you're doing *to* us, like the way you pushed around Thad Cooper last night."

"Oh, hell, that weren't nothin'."

"It'd better not happen again."

Sheriff Rawlins narrowed his eyes. "Don't threaten me, less'n you're prepared to back it up."

"We won't tolerate endless abuse from you, Rawlins. Don't push us too far. We're not as helpless as you might think."

Sheriff Rawlins laughed, and Mayor Randlett walked out of the office. When he closed the door, a few shards of glass broke loose and fell to the floor.

"Ain't that a kick in the ass," Sheriff Rawlins said to Pritchard. "Them bastards get persnickety over every little thing."

"Slapping a member of the town council isn't such a little thing," Pritchard said.

"Them bastards need somebody to wake 'em up every now and then."

Rawlins arose and went to the file cabinet, pulling out an armful of wanted posters. He dropped them to his desk and began going through them, sipping from his whiskey bottle.

Jennifer looked up from her desk as her father entered the office. "What happened?"

"He's a hard man," he replied. "I don't know what we're going to do with him."

"What'd he say about Thad Cooper?"

"He more or less said he's got a right to push people around if he feels like it."

"You've got to get rid of him, Daddy. You know he's not going to get any better. He'll only get worse."

Mayor Randlett ran his hand over his short gray beard. "He was drinking whiskey out of a bottle while he was talking to me. It was really quite amazing, but I'm afraid he's got us over a barrel. If we fire him, who'll protect us?"

"What about John Stone?"

The door to the office opened, and Mayor Randlett turned around. He was astonished to see John Stone enter, a bruise on his mouth and his eyes puffy from lack of sleep.

"Well, well, well," Mayor Randlett said, slapping Stone on the shoulder. "We were just talking about you. Are you all right?"

"I'm living in the Olympia Hotel," Stone said groggily, "and I can't sleep. It's just too damned noisy, and they can't give me a quieter room because the hotel's full right now. I just thought

I should tell you that if I can't find a quiet place to sleep pretty soon, I'm probably not going to stay here for a month, as I'd promised."

Mayor Randlett rubbed his hands together. "You came to the right place. I own quite a lot of real estate in this town, and I'm sure we can find something for you"—he turned to his daughter—"can't we, dear?"

"Of course," Jennifer said, thinking swiftly, and then she smiled graciously at Stone, "and until we do, Deputy Stone, you can stay in the guest room at our house, isn't that right, Daddy?"

"Um . . . well . . . I . . . certainly." Mayor Randlett didn't want to disagree with his daughter in front of Stone.

Jennifer looked up at Stone. "Just go to our house and tell Esmeralda—she's our maid—to let you have the guest room. I'm sure you'll find it very peaceful. We live in a quiet part of the town."

"I couldn't do that," Stone said, his voice deep and dull from fatigue.

"Why not?" asked Jennifer.

"I wouldn't want to put you to any trouble."

"No trouble at all, is it Daddy?"

"Ah . . . no, none."

"Then it's settled," Jennifer said. She explained to Stone where the house was, on the hill at the eastern end of town. "Make yourself at home. If you get hungry, just tell Esmeralda what you want."

Stone was so tired he was ready to do anything to get some sleep. "This is very kind of you."

"It's our pleasure to help you out. After all, we're grateful for all you've done for us, aren't we, Daddy?"

"Why . . . uh . . . yes."

Jennifer turned to Stone. "I'm sure you'll be comfortable with us, and we'd love to have you."

"I'll stay with you until I can find a suitable place of my own."

Her green eyes glittered like emeralds. "You may stay as long as you like, Captain Stone."

Stone thanked her and her father, and backed out of the office, closing the door behind him.

It was silent in the office for a few moments, and Mayor Randlett stared at his daughter as if seeing her for the first time. She calmly picked up a land lease and looked it over, as if nothing unusual had happened.

"Young lady," Mayor Randlett said, "what are you up to?"

She maintained her gaze on the lease. "I'm afraid I don't know what you're talking about, Daddy."

"I think you're being disingenuous, my dear, but you can't fool me. I used to change your diapers. Could you please tell me what in the world is going on between you and Captain Stone?"

"The poor man needs a place to sleep, that's all."

Mayor Randlett wrinkled his brow and tried to imagine Stone as a woman might see him. "Are you in love with him, in some way?" he asked her.

"Why, Daddy, I hardly know him!"

"Don't do anything foolish, Jennifer."

"But, Daddy, all I did was offer our deputy sheriff a place to sleep. Whatever can you be talking about?"

"You know very well what I'm talking about. Just be careful, that's all. John Stone is a drifter and we really don't know very much about him. Sheriff Rawlins thinks he might be a wanted man."

"Sheriff Rawlins is an obnoxious drunkard and everybody knows it. Why anybody pays attention to him is beyond me."

"Just be careful," he told her, "and now, if you'll excuse me, I've got work to do."

"I just thought of something, Daddy. What if Esmeralda doesn't let Captain Stone into the house? I mean, she doesn't know him from Adam. She might think he's a burglar. Maybe I'd better run home quickly and tell her to expect him."

Mayor Randlett looked askance at his daughter. "If you like," he said.

She stood behind her desk, smoothed the folds of her skirt, and headed for the door. Mayor Randlett watched her tall, slim figure, her flashing red hair. *Only nineteen years old*, he thought. *It's a dangerous age.*

Jennifer walked swiftly down the main street of Petie, the sun gleaming on her brilliant red hair. Men tipped their hats and said hello, and she smiled back perfunctorily, but her mind was somewhere else.

She was thinking about John Stone, wondering if she'd gone too far when she'd invited him to stay at her home. Would he be aware that she liked him?

I shouldn't be so impetuous, she said to herself. *I don't want him to think I'm throwing myself at him. Men don't respect women who throw themselves at them.*

She recalled how he'd looked, sleepy and grumpy, in her father's office. He was a big strong man, but he needed a woman to take care of him, that was clear to her, and she thought she might be the right woman for him, although she couldn't be sure.

She barely knew him, after all. It was premature to think of marriage, but there was something about John Stone that excited her. She thought him handsome and charming, and could feel the strength of his body all the way across a room. He made her nervous, and no man ever had made her nervous before.

I've got to be calm whenever I'm with him, she said to herself. *I can't ever let him know what I'm thinking or feeling. Somehow I've got to make him come to me.*

Out on the prairie, near the base of the Hawksridge Mountains, Deke Casey and his men were gathered around their breakfast fire, drinking harsh black coffee and smoking cigarettes.

"We don't all want to ride into Petie together," Casey said, spreading a crude map of the town and its surrounding territory on the ground, "so I'll go in first with Schuler, and we'll take a look around, find out what happened to Chopak. We'll meet up with the rest of you after sundown here," he pointed to a hill to the west of town. "Hurley, you and Ramsay'll carry the dynamite for the bank. Anybody got any questions?"

Nobody said anything, and Casey tossed the butt of his cigarette into the fire. He nodded to Schuler and they arose, walking back toward the horses. He'd selected Schuler because Schuler was the fastest gun in the outfit. If there was any trouble in Petie, he'd rather have Schuler at his side than any other of his men.

Casey and Schuler climbed onto their horses and rode away,

heading for Petie. The other outlaws put out the fire and broke camp, preparing for their own journey to Petie later that morning. Their mood was solemn and mean. John Stone had killed eight of their comrades, maybe nine if he'd got Chopak, and that night they were going to pay him back.

They'd surround him, shoot him down like a dog, and watch him die. Maybe they could gutshoot him, so he'd die slowly, or shoot off his kneecaps, which was the most painful wound of all.

But no matter how they shot him, he was going to die.

John Stone stood in front of the Randlett mansion, a saddlebag full of his belongings in his left hand and his rifle in his right hand. The mansion was large and white, two stories high, and had Georgian columns in front, reminding him of the home in which he'd grown up back in South Carolina before the war.

His home had been substantially larger than this one, and the architecture had been finer, in his opinion. Albemarle had been situated on a hill, and a visitor approached the front door on a long, winding road lined with leafy oak trees. There were vast lawns dotted with trees and bushes, and many slaves labored to keep them neat and well manicured. Not far away were forests full of game, where Stone had hunted during the day, and at night there were fabulous parties, with full orchestras and ladies dressed in the most beautiful gowns. Stone had never done a lick of work in his life until he went to West Point. He'd been a rich man's son and never had lacked anything. Then the war came, the Confederacy was crushed, and now Stone was just another saddle bum, roaming the frontier.

He knocked on the front door and waited for a few moments. All he wanted to do was get to bed as soon as possible.

The door was opened and he saw Jennifer Randlett standing in front of him. "Come right in," she said. "I had to come home to take care of a few things, and I might as well show you your room." She turned around and shouted, "Esmeralda!"

A stout black maid in a white apron entered the vestibule, and she reminded Stone of his old mammy back at Albemarle. He removed his hat.

"Esmeralda, this is John Stone, our new deputy sheriff. He'll be staying with us for a while. Please see that he gets anything he wants." She turned to Stone. "This way, Captain. I'll show you your room."

He followed her into the living room, where a huge crystal chandelier hung over their heads, and up the curving staircase to the second floor. He was aware of her perfume trailing behind her, and she lifted her skirts as she climbed the stairs, revealing her trim ankles.

She led him to a room on the second floor, and they went inside. It had white wallpaper and large windows overlooking the mountains in the distance. The bed was immense, covered with a white ruffled bedspread, and above the bed was a painting of a herd of mustangs galloping over the prairie. Jennifer opened the window, and a cool breeze touched Stone's cheeks.

She turned around and smiled. "Hope you like it. If you need anything, just call Esmeralda. Now if you'll excuse me, I've got to be going. Oh, yes—one more thing—do you think you'd like to have dinner with us this evening?"

"I go on duty at eight."

"Dinner will be served at six-thirty. That should give you plenty of time. Is there anything you don't like to eat?"

"I eat anything."

"We'll expect you for dinner at six-thirty, then. I hope you're able to get some sleep here."

"I'm sure I won't have any trouble."

She turned and left the room. Stone stripped off his shirt, then washed his hands and face in the basin, thinking of Jennifer. She certainly was a lively little thing, quite vivacious and pretty. In a way, she reminded him of Marie, who also had been bright and full of life.

He dried himself with the big fluffy towel and pulled the drapes over the window, blocking out the light, plunging the room into darkness. He removed the remainder of his clothing and crawled into bed, bringing his head to rest on the pillow. He closed his eyes, remembering Jennifer's brilliant red hair.

Deke Casey and Fritz Schuler hitched their horses to the rail in front of the Paradise Saloon. They looked to the left and right, and Casey angled his head toward the front of the saloon.

They climbed to the sidewalk, pushed the doors, and stepped

inside. Both had been here before when they'd been planning the bank robbery, and they headed for the bar.

"Whiskey," said Casey.

Doreen Eckles was working behind the bar. She placed a bottle of whiskey and two glasses in front of them.

"Nice day," she said with a smile, trying to make conversation.

"Yeah," grunted Casey.

She realized they didn't want to talk with her and moved to another part of the bar. She wasn't surprised, cowboys and freighters were often a moody lot, probably because they spent so much time alone on the prairie.

Casey raised the glass to his lips and took a sip. His hat had a cord that hung around his neck, and a one-inch length of hollow bone could tighten or loosen the cord. He pulled the bone down all the way and pushed the hat off his head, causing the hat to hang behind him, showing his straight black hair streaked with a few strands of gray.

He and Schuler were dirty and unshaven, but so were many of the other drinkers in the saloon. He leaned his back against the bar and looked at the men playing cards. If things were different, he wouldn't mind sitting in on a game.

A waitress walked by, carrying a tray of drinks. Casey turned to her and licked his upper lip. It'd been a long time since he'd had a woman, and he undressed her with his eyes. If the bank robbery had worked, he and his men would've taken the money and gone to a whorehouse.

Casey and Schuler stood at the bar and had a few drinks, looking at the waitresses, listening to conversations, trying to find out what was going on. A man with a big belly, wearing a suit with the coat open, approached the bar.

"Whiskey," he said.

Doreen placed a bottle and glass in front of him.

"Nice town you got here," he told Doreen. "I been in some towns lately that I wouldn't give you a dime for."

"Travel a lot?" asked Doreen.

"I'm a salesman. Sell to dry-goods stores. Carry a nice line of ladies' garments. Like to show 'em to you sometime."

Doreen had heard every line in the book, and this one wasn't new. "Maybe later," she said.

"Best thing about this town," the salesman continued, "is that it's so peaceful. I always like to come here. Never feel like somebody's gonna shoot me when I'm not looking."

"You should've been here last night," Doreen said. "We had plenty of shootin'. Our new deputy sheriff, John Stone, had to kill a drunk who went crazy at Miss Elsie's, and then a stranger tried to bushwhack Stone, but Stone shot him first."

Casey leaned his elbow on the bar and smiled, showing tobacco-stained teeth. "Who tried to bushwhack your deputy?" he asked Doreen.

"Nobody ever seen him before yesterday. He was a big feller, had a tattoo on his arm."

Casey looked at Schuler significantly. They picked up their glasses and bottle of whiskey and made their way to one of the empty tables, sitting down across from each other. Casey propped up his feet on an empty chair.

"Guess we don't have to worry about Chopak no more," he said.

"Always was a damn fool," Schuler replied. "I bet I could've taken Stone. Would've walked straight up to him and drawed."

Casey looked at Schuler, who wore long blond sideburns and had a pink complexion. "Maybe he would've been faster than you."

"There's only one way to find out."

"What the hell's the point of takin' a chance, when you could have a sure thing?"

Schuler leaned toward Casey and grinned. "I like to see a man's face when I shoot him. They always look surprised, as if they can't believe it's happening to 'em."

"You think you could take John Stone?"

"Sure."

"What makes you think so?"

"Ain't many faster than me."

"What if he's one of them?"

Schuler shrugged. "We're all gonna die sooner or later."

"Look who's here," said Schuler.

Schuler turned around and saw Sheriff Rawlins walk into the Paradise, his fingers hitched in his belt. He wore his customary frock coat that reached his knees, and his black hat with the flat crown. The only open spot at the bar was next to the salesman, and Rawlins stepped beside him, placing his foot on the rail.

"Whiskey!" he called out loudly.

The salesman turned to him and smiled. "Howdy, Sheriff. Heard your deputy had a hot time for himself last night."

Rawlins looked at him and narrowed his eyes. "Who're you?"

"Name's Smith, and I'm a traveling salesman. Pleased to make your acquaintance."

Smith held out his hand, to shake with Rawlins, but Rawlins looked at his hand disdainfully, and Smith withdrew it. Meanwhile, Doreen brought Rawlins his whiskey and filled his glass half full, just the way he liked it. Rawlins raised the glass and gulped it down.

Smith watched him with admiration. He knew of Rawlins's reputation, and people in other towns that he'd visited spoke of Rawlins in the same breath that they spoke of the great gunfighters of the frontier. Rawlins was a legend, and Smith was proud to be standing next to him.

"Guess it's nice to have a new deputy," Smith said, trying to strike up a conversation with the great man.

Rawlins didn't say anything. He just poured himself another half glass of whiskey.

"What happened last night anyway?"

Rawlins threw his head back and drank the whiskey, his Adam's apple bobbing up and down.

"Guess your new deputy takes some of the load off your shoulders. Wish I had somebody to take the load off my shoulders. It ain't easy carrying a bag of samples all over the damned countryside. Sell men's clothes too, by the way. You might want to look at some of my merchandise. Bring a few items over to your office anytime you like. Just tell me when." Smith smiled. "I aim to please."

Rawlins turned to him, and his eyes were bloodshot. "Get away from me," he said, a deadly tone in his voice.

The smile vanished off the salesman's face. "Didn't mean any harm, Sheriff. Just making conversation."

"Hit the road."

The bar became still, and the salesman was aware that all eyes were on him, but he'd always been a fast talker and was confident he could talk his way out of anything.

"Sure thing, Sheriff," he said with a smile. "Just as soon as I finish my drink."

In a sudden lunging movement, Rawlins spun the salesman around, grabbed him by his collar and the seat of his pants, and carried him to the doors, while the salesman screamed and flailed his arms helplessly. Rawlins kicked the doors open and heaved the salesman into the middle of the street.

The salesman flew through the air, his legs kicking wildly, his mouth agape with fear, and landed in the muck. Rawlins turned around and reentered the saloon, and everybody was laughing. He returned to his position at the bar and poured himself another drink.

A few feet away, a freighter was giggling in his beer. He had a droopy mustache and had just arrived in town. Rawlins looked at him.

"What's yer problem!"

The freighter went pale. "I got no problem, Sheriff."

"Stop that goddamned noise."

The saloon went silent. Rawlins picked up his glass. Across the room, Deke Casey leaned toward Fritz Schuler and said softly, "Think you could handle Rawlins?"

"Sure."

"They say he's awful fast."

"Maybe he was awful fast in his prime, but he ain't in his prime no more. He looks like a goddamn drunk to me. He pushes me around, I'll show him what fast is."

The door to the office opened, and Jennifer looked up. She saw a middle-aged man covered with mud from head to foot.

"Can I help you?" Jennifer asked.

"I'd like to speak with the mayor."

"I'm afraid he's busy right now. Is there anything I can do?"

"It's about your sheriff. Look what he did to me."

Smith gazed down at his clothes. They were wet and filthy, but more than that his pride was hurt. He considered himself a clever person, and it had been humiliating to be laughed at by everybody in sight.

"What exactly did he do to you?" Jennifer asked.

"He threw me in the street."

"What for?"

"I was only being friendly, and before I knew it, he attacked me. Let me tell you something, young lady. I do a lot of traveling, and I've seen a lot of sheriffs. They're supposed to help people, and uphold law and order, not attack honest citizens who pay their taxes and mind their own business. I think something ought to be done about your sheriff, before he actually harms an innocent person."

"I'll take it up with the mayor," Jennifer said.

"The man's a menace to life and property. I've never been treated this way in my life."

"The mayor will receive a full report."

The salesman filled his lungs with air and expelled it loudly. He was angry and didn't know what to do. Frustrated and embarrassed, he considered it unmanly to complain to a woman. Turning around, he walked out of the office.

A few seconds after he left, the door behind Jennifer opened and her father stepped out.

"Rawlins is at it again," he said, frowning, because he'd heard everything. "What in the name of God am I going to do with him?"

"You're going to fire him, Daddy," Jennifer said pertly. "That's what you're going to do with him."

"That man who was just in here—I know who he is. He comes to town regularly—I've seen him before. He's a traveling salesman for one of the big companies out east, and wherever he goes from now on, he's going to tell everybody that Rawlins is a drunk and a ruffian, and he'll warn people not to come to Petie because of Rawlins. It's just the kind of thing that can hurt the economic development of this town. We need people to say good things about us, not bad things."

"When are you going to fire Sheriff Rawlins, Daddy?"

"I don't know," Randlett said, looking perplexed, "but I suppose I'll have to do it soon. We can't tolerate much more of this kind of behavior from Rawlins. It's just too darn undignified, and what's worse, it's bad for business."

"Out of my way, goddamn it!" said Rawlins.

He stood impatiently in front of his office, and a workman was installing a new plate of glass into the door. The workman stepped hastily out of his way, and Rawlins opened the door, charging into the room.

He didn't bother to take off his hat, as he sat behind his desk. Pritchard looked at him curiously. Rawlins seemed to be in an unusual state of agitation.

Rawlins's desk was piled high with wanted posters. Earlier in the day he'd emptied out all the file cabinets and boxes, and some of the wanted posters were twenty years old, yellowed and tattered, falling apart.

Rawlins had gone through all the posters and hadn't found anybody that resembled John Stone. That's why he'd been in an unusually rotten mood when he'd gone to the Paradise Saloon. If he hadn't been in such a mood, he might've left the salesman alone.

But he'd noticed something in the Paradise, and it set off a spark in his brain. About ten years ago, Rawlins had been passing through the town of Lanesboro, and they'd had a certain outlaw in jail. This outlaw had robbed a stagecoach and been caught by the local sheriff's posse. Sheriff Rawlins stopped by the Lanesboro jail to pick up his own prisoner, and got a good look at close range at the outlaw. Two weeks later, after having returned to Petie, he'd learned that the outlaw had been busted out of jail by members of his gang. They'd attacked the jail in the middle of the night and blown down a wall with dynamite.

Rawlins had forgotten about the incident, but now it was in the forefront of his mind again, because *he'd seen that outlaw just now in the Paradise Saloon*. The outlaw had been sitting at a table with a man who wore long blond sideburns. Rawlins may've been a drunk and a bully, but he'd been a lawman for twenty years and never forgot a face.

He searched through the wanted posters again, because he recalled coming across the picture of the outlaw earlier in the day when he'd been looking for John Stone. He hadn't paid any particular attention to it at the time, because it had no relevance to John Stone. It registered quickly in his mind that it was of the outlaw he'd seen in the Lanesboro jail, and he'd passed it by.

His brows furrowed in concentration, he thumbed through the piles of posters again. He'd forgotten the outlaw's name, and exactly in which pile the picture had been. Five piles of posters sat on his desk, and he'd just have to go through them all again. The life of a lawman wasn't all gunfighting in the middle of the street. A lot of it was boring detail work that the average citizen didn't even know about.

That's what made him hate John Stone. Stone had managed to break up one bank robbery, and somehow he was the hero of the town, while Rawlins had given his life to Petie.

Rawlins knew he was getting old, and knew he was a drunkard, but he thought he still was ten times more man than John Stone. Somehow he had to prove that to the people of Petie.

Slowly he searched through the wanted posters. His eyes blurred over and occasionally he had to take a drink from his bottle to fortify himself. A parade of faces passed in front of him, and they were young and old, wore hats or were bareheaded, had dark hair or light hair, but each and every one had a sinister expression on his face, men who'd cut your throat for a dime.

Finally, in the third pile, he saw him. It was the same long face and thin mouth he'd seen at the Paradise. Rawlins picked up the wanted poster and held it up to the light, so he could see better.

He was wanted dead or alive, and his name was Deke Casey. A five-hundred-dollar reward was offered. He was leader of an outlaw band that committed murder, stagecoach holdups, bank robberies, and cattle rustling.

Bank Robberies. Rawlins flashed on the bank robbery that Stone had broken up yesterday. Had Deke Casey been mixed up in that? Rawlins took out a stogie and lit it up, puffing until his head disappeared in blue smoke. Could it be that Deke Casey was going to try to rob the Petie Savings Bank again?

Rawlins had been friends with outlaws in the days before he became a lawman. He'd drunk and gambled with them, gone whoring with them, and occasionally had rustled cattle with them. He knew how they thought, and tried to put himself into Deke Casey's mind.

It hit him like a slap in the face. John Stone had killed eight bank robbers yesterday, and if they'd been Deke Casey's men, Deke Casey would want revenge. Outlaws had their own warped code of justice. Maybe Deke Casey was in town to kill John Stone.

Rawlins puffed his cigarette. He ought to warn Stone, and he and Stone should arrest Casey without delay. If they managed it right, they could take Casey with a minimum of trouble. It was the proper thing to do.

But Rawlins knew what'd happen if he and Stone captured Deke Casey. The mood of the citizens being what it was, Stone probably would get all the credit, while Rawlins's role would be denigrated.

The alternative would be for him to go back to the Paradise alone right now, put his gun in Deke Casey's face, and place him under arrest.

That'd be dangerous, because Deke Casey probably wouldn't surrender quietly, and he hadn't been alone. He'd been sitting with a young man with blond hair who'd been giving Rawlins dirty looks. There'd be gunplay, no doubt about that, but Rawlins thought he could handle it. He'd handled worse in the past.

But why should he risk his life for John Stone? Rawlins realized that if he arrested Deke Casey, the townspeople wouldn't respect him any more than they did now. They expected him to arrest people. It was his job. They were so used to his protection and skill that they took him for granted.

Rawlins leaned back in his chair and puffed his stogie. Maybe he should let Deke Casey kill John Stone, and then, after the smoke cleared, Rawlins would arrest Casey. Then the townspeople would be forced to see, right before their eyes, that John Stone was really nothing more than a flash in the pan, and that he, Sheriff Buck Rawlins, was the better man.

Rawlins knew he was embarking on a hazardous course whose outcome couldn't be accurately predicted. A man like Deke Casey wasn't anybody to fool with. But Rawlins thought he'd take the chance. Although he hated the townspeople, he wanted them to respect him. This was the strange paradox of his alcoholic life, and it pushed him over the edge.

I'll just stay in the background and keep my eyes open, he thought. *Let John Stone look out for himself, if he thinks he's so smart.*

5

JOHN STONE OPENED his eyes, and at first he didn't know where he was. He was accustomed to waking up on the prairie, with the sky above and his head on his saddle, wearing the clothes he'd worn the day before, bearded and filthy, or he'd wake up in a small hotel room in a strange town he'd never been in before, but now he was in a luxurious large bedroom, and everything was white.

He got out of bed and walked to the window, pulling the drapes to the side. The sun was low on the horizon; it was late in the afternoon.

He felt well rested and strong, and his headache was gone. Sitting on the bed again, he rolled his first cigarette of the day.

There was a knock on the door. "Captain Stone?" asked Esmeralda the maid.

"What is it?" he asked.

"Dinner will be served in a half hour, Captain Stone."

He washed his face and hands and rinsed out his mouth. Then he shaved with his straight razor. It was a pretty good razor, but not as good as the one his father had given him when he went away to West Point. That razor had been lost long ago during the war, when they'd had to abandon a position quickly and leave everything behind.

He tried not to think too much of his mother and father, because it was too painful, and the pain distracted him from whatever he had to do. They'd died of illness and heartbreak within a few weeks of each other after the plantation had been burned to the ground by Sherman's army toward the end of the war. Stone had found out about it in a letter he'd received from Marie shortly before the battle of Sayler's Creek. He couldn't go home, because he couldn't walk away from his cavalry troop when it was at the front, but many a Union soldier had dropped beneath his flashing saber during the fight that followed, and that had been his revenge.

Now he had no more rancor left. Unlike others, he'd spent all his on the field of battle for four long bloody years. Now all he wanted to do was find Marie and put his life back together again.

He reached for his gunbelts, but stopped his hands in midair. He was going to dinner with civilized people; there was no need to wear guns. To be on the safe side, he dropped his knife into its sheath in his boot.

He looked at himself in the mirror and saw a tall man with his dark blond hair worn short and parted neatly on the left side, just like when he was in the army. He didn't suppose he'd changed much since then, except the lines in his face were a little deeper, and his body had filled somewhat.

He left his room and descended the stairs to the first floor of the house. The sun streamed through the windows and Jennifer Randlett walked toward him from the dining room. She wore a long gown, and her eyes were sparkling.

"Did you sleep well?" she asked.

"Like a baby."

They entered the dining room, and the table was set for three. Mayor Randlett, wearing a suit and tie, appeared through another doorway, carrying a bottle of whiskey.

"Care for a drink?" he asked Stone.

"Please."

Mayor Randlett poured the drink and handed it to Stone. "I propose a toast," he said. "To our new deputy sheriff—John Stone!"

He touched his glass to Stone's, and both of the men drank. Mayor Randlett sat at one end of the table, Stone at the other, and Jennifer in the middle with her back to the window. It was a long table and a considerable distance separated each of them.

Esmeralda brought out the tureen of soup and placed it on the table. She took Stone's bowl and filled it with steaming chicken broth. Then she served Jennifer and Mayor Randlett. Stone kept glancing surreptitiously at Jennifer. She was really an extraordinarily pretty woman, he realized.

He waited for her to taste her soup, then dipped his spoon in his bowl. It was delicious, so different from the restaurant food he usually ate, or the stuff he wolfed down on the trail. Like so many other aspects of the Randlett mansion, it reminded him of Albemarle, where he'd eaten like a prince three meals a day all his life until he'd left for West Point at the age of eighteen.

"Sorry you had a bad night," Mayor Randlett said. "Hope you're not discouraged with your job."

"We'll see how tonight goes."

"Should be easier. This isn't a bad town. I hate to say it, but the biggest law and order problem we have in this town, as a rule, is our sheriff, of all people. Last night he slapped a member of the town council, name of Thad Cooper, at the Paradise Saloon, and today he threw a visitor bodily into the middle of the street. I understand he behaved provocatively toward you too."

"Nothing serious."

"I disagree with you. I think it's very serious. A sheriff is supposed to be the paragon of law and order in a town, not the worst troublemaker of all. To tell you the truth, Captain Stone, I and other members of the town council want to get rid of Rawlins. He's an embarrassment to everybody and a threat to public safety. The problem is that we can't let him go unless we have a good man to replace him with."

"Don't look at me," Stone said.

"Why not?"

"I don't know anything about being a lawman. Last night I realized how unqualified I really am. I'll last out the month if I can, because I gave you my word that I would, but I'm not crazy about the job. Sheriff Rawlins seems to be maintaining law and order fairly well, although he's not an easy man to deal with. I'd suggest you think twice about firing him."

"We could make it a very attractive proposition financially, you know," Mayor Randlett said.

"Money will be of no use to me in the cemetery, and that's where I'll wind up if I become your sheriff." He looked at Mayor Randlett. "Do you have any idea how dangerous that job is? Do you know what it's like to confront angry drunken men who're armed to the teeth? I know Rawlins is a drunkard, but he's held the job for twenty years and made this town as safe as any on the frontier. I think you should give him the extra money, not me."

Mayor Randlett and his daughter looked at each other.

"Sorry you feel that way," Mayor Randlett said to Stone. "I don't want to be overbearing, but we'd really like you to stay. Are you sure there's nothing we could do to change your mind? We're prepared to go to considerable lengths to retain you."

"No chance," Stone replied. "Sorry."

Jennifer gave her father another look, and he gave up. In silence, the three of them ate their chicken soup. Stone continued to glance at Jennifer out of the corner of his eye. He'd noticed the silent communication between her and her father, and realized that his red-haired young beauty had a lot to say about what went on in Petie, but most people probably didn't know it.

She was a beautiful young woman and someday she'd inherit all her father's vast holdings. *The man who marries her will be a lucky son of a gun*, he thought. She glanced at him, and he looked down at his food. *I'd better not think about her too much*, he said to himself, *otherwise I'm liable to get in more trouble than I'm in already*.

Rawlins stomped into the Paradise Saloon, scanned the tables quickly, and made his way to the bar.

"Whiskey."

He was looking for Deke Casey, to keep track of him, but Deke Casey wasn't there. Rawlins downed a glass of whiskey, left the Paradise, and walked to the Acme, pushing through the swinging doors.

"Whiskey."

He looked around, trying not to be obvious, but Deke Casey wasn't here either. Had he left town? What the hell was going on?

He drained his glass, wiped his mouth with the back of his hand, and walked outside. He thought he'd search the town, first one side of the street and then the other.

He made his way down the sidewalk, his gait steady although he'd been drinking since he got out of bed that morning. Stopping in front of Bob's Barbershop, he struck a match against the side of the building and lit a stogie. Then he continued his search, and men stepped out of his way. Some crossed to the other side of the street to avoid him. Nobody wanted a run-in with Sheriff Rawlins.

He was courteous to ladies, touching his finger to the brim of his hat and muttering something friendly whenever he passed one of them. He'd been taught to respect women, but their husbands and brothers were liars and low schemers, in his opinion.

He spotted Casey, sitting on the bench in front of the hardware store. Rawlins didn't slow down or give any sign that he'd seen Casey. He just kept walking, passing him and the blond man sitting beside him, but Rawlins's senses were wide awake, and he was listening for the click of a hammer being cocked. If he heard it, he was prepared to spin around and send forth a hail of lead.

But there was no click of a hammer, and Rawlins kept moving on. Schuler turned to Casey and smirked. "Fuckin' old fool," he said.

"Don't underestimate Buck Rawlins," Casey said. "He's a tough old bird."

"Don't look so tough to me."

"We don't want a run-in with him. It's John Stone we want."

Deke Casey turned and looked at Rawlins's back as the sheriff of Petie moved farther away on the boardwalk. Casey wasn't aware that he'd seen Rawlins in the Lanesboro jail ten years ago. A lot of lawmen had been on the scene, coming and going, and Rawlins hadn't stood out in his mind. A good memory wasn't one of Deke Casey's strong points, but he was able to plan robberies like military operations and bring them off successfully most of the time.

"John Stone should be comin' on duty pretty soon," Casey said. "Keep yer eyes open for him."

"The man who shoots John Stone would be famous," Schuler replied. "He'd git his name in the papers."

"Forget about it," Casey told him. "Don't be a damn fool all yer life."

"You don't think I can take him?"

"I don't know if you could or not, but we're not gonna play it that way."

"It'd be the easiest way. I'd just egg him on and shoot him down."

"You really think you could take him?"

"I know I could."

"What makes you so sure?"

"I never run into nobody faster than me yet."

"There's always the first time."

"John Stone just had one lucky day, that's all. Lemme draw on him, Deke. It's the bestest way to git rid of him. If all of us try it at the same time, it'll be too messy."

Casey looked at Schuler, who wasn't the first fast gun he'd known in his life, and they all had the same trait, an eagerness to test themselves again and again in the most dangerous competition of all. But Schuler was right when he said it'd be messy if all of them tried to shoot Stone down at the same time. Maybe he should let Schuler do the dirty work. It certainly would be easier that way.

"I'll think it over," Casey said.

Schuler smiled. He could see that Casey was moving closer to his position. He reached down to his Colt and wrapped his fingers around the barrel. *John Stone*, he thought, *you're as good as dead*.

In his luxurious bedroom, John Stone strapped on his two gunbelts. He put on his hat and left the room, descending the stairs to the main floor of the mansion.

He entered the vestibule, and Esmeralda opened the front door for him. Stone stopped in front of her and gazed down at her face. "You know, you look an awful lot like my old mammy," he said in his southern drawl. "Been meaning to tell you that."

"Was she good to you?" Esmeralda asked.

"I loved her with all my heart."

Esmeralda beamed, and Stone walked out the door. He crossed the veranda and descended the steps that led to the walkway, on the way to his second night as deputy sheriff of Petie.

It was dark, and another full moon hung in the sky over the mountains in the distance. Stone was thinking about the discussion he'd had with Mayor Randlett and Jennifer at the dinner table earlier. It was clear that they wanted to oust Sheriff Rawlins and install him, John Stone, as sheriff. He knew the Randletts would continue their efforts to recruit him, and he wouldn't be able to get away from their pressure because he was living underneath their roof.

There was another problem with living in the Randlett mansion, and that was Jennifer herself. She was a pretty little thing, and Stone was attracted to her. He thought she was attracted to him too. Sooner or later they'd be alone together in a room of the mansion, and anything could happen.

Stone didn't want anything to happen, because he was engaged to Marie. *I've got to find another place to live*, he thought.

He was reluctant to move out of the Randlett mansion, because he loved the luxury, but he'd have to move out if he wanted to get some peace of mind. *I'll ask around tonight. Should be able to find something suitable.*

In a few minutes he was in the center of Petie, approaching the door of the sheriff's office, and he noticed that the new window had been installed. The door was unlocked and he pushed it open, seeing Buck Rawlins seated behind his desk. The other desk was vacant; Pritchard had gone home for the day.

"Evening, Sheriff," Stone said, trying to be friendly.

Rawlins looked up from the shotgun he was cleaning on his desk. "What the hell you think you was doin' last night?" he asked roughly. "A lawman don't git into brawls with people. When that cowpoke took a broken bottle on you, you should've shot him. You ain't afraid to shoot somebody, are you?"

"Yesterday when I asked you what the job involved, you wouldn't tell me anything."

"I ain't yer nursemaid. If you didn't know nothin' about the job, you shouldn't've took it."

"I needed the money."

Rawlins snapped his shotgun together and glowered at Stone. "You want my job, don't you?"

"I'm leaving this town as soon as my month is up."

Rawlins snorted. Without another word or even a glance at Stone, he picked up the shotgun and headed for the door.

He left Stone alone in the office. Rawlins's desk was cleared; all the wanted posters had been put away. Stone wondered how his prisoners were doing. He took the keys from the notch and unlocked the door to the jail area.

He found the two prisoners together in the dark, damp cell. One had his arm bandaged and lay with his eyes closed on his cot, his face pale. The other sat on his cot with his back to the wall and looked sideways at Stone.

The man's face was badly bruised, and both his eyes had been blackened. He looked at Stone with undisguised hatred.

Stone returned to the outer office and was about to sit behind Pritchard's desk when the door opened. He looked up and saw Toby Muldoon, broken guitar in hand.

"Miss Elsie wants to palaver with you," Muldoon said, "but it ain't no emergency."

Stone didn't have anything pressing to do, and thought he might as well walk over there before he got busy.

"I'll see her now," he said.

He and Muldoon stepped outside into the darkness, and Stone locked the door.

"Buy me a drink?" Muldoon asked.

Stone handed him some coins, and they parted. Stone headed toward the north end of town where Miss Elsie's establishment was located. He hadn't gone ten steps when he was accosted by Mabel Billings, president of the Ladies Auxiliary at the Petie Church of God.

"We're expecting you in church this Sunday, Captain Stone," she said, wagging her forefinger before him, and it looked like a sausage.

"I'll be there if I can make it," he replied.

"Nobody should be too busy to attend worship," she admonished him. "We also hope you plan to attend our Harvest Moon Ball."

He told her he didn't know anything about the Harvest Moon Ball, and she proceeded to explain it in detail. He listened politely, but finally, after several minutes, couldn't handle it anymore.

"I'm sorry, but I've got to get going," he told her. "I have to see somebody on the other end of town."

"We'll be looking for you at the Harvest Moon Ball," she said.

He tipped his hat and headed for Miss Elsie's place again, hoping he hadn't been rude. He realized that Jennifer almost certainly would attend the Harvest Moon Ball, since she was the mayor's daughter, and he'd probably wind up dancing with her. Maybe he'd better start figuring out an excuse so he wouldn't have to go to the bll, because he didn't want the temptation. Jennifer was too pretty and he was too lonely, a dangerous combination.

"This must be him," Deke Casey said.

Casey and Schuler were sitting on the bench in front of the tobacconist, and they looked at Stone approaching on the sidewalk. Casey had never seen him before, but he spotted the tin badge.

"I could take him down right now," Schuler said, his fingers closing around the handle of his gun.

"Don't look at him. We don't want to make him suspicious."

Casey and Schuler tilted their hats over their faces and leaned back, as if they were taking a nap. Stone barely noticed them as he walked by; he was thinking about Jennifer Randlett.

They waited until he'd passed, then pushed their hats back and looked at his broad shoulders and the two guns on his hips as he merged with the darkness and disappeared.

"Looks like he knows what he's about," Casey said.

"I want him," Schuler said.

"You might be gittin' in over yer head."

Casey considered himself a good judge of men. Stone seemed tough and confident, nobody to take lightly. Men usually didn't exude that kind of confidence unless they had something to back it up.

"You don't think I'm fast?" Schuler asked.

"I know you're fast."

"I wanna draw on him."

"Let me think about it."

"What if I didn't care what you thought about it, Deke? What if I just went and did it myself?"

Casey looked at Schuler, whose eyes were bright with excitement, as if he'd just seen a pretty girl.

"How come you want to fight him so bad?"

"I wanna see how fast he is."

"What if he's faster than you?"

"He ain't."

"How do you know?"

"I know."

Casey wondered if Schuler really was as confident as he appeared, or if he was just trying to convince himself. Schuler had always seemed a little erratic, but there was no doubt that he was fast. Casey had seen him kill before.

"I want to draw on him," Schuler said, squeezing the handle of his gun. "I want to show everybody who's fastest."

"We got plenty of time," Casey replied. "Let's go have a drink."

The outlaws arose, and walked down the boardwalk to the Paradise Saloon. Across the street, two beady little eyes watched them. They belonged to Toby Muldoon, sprawled on a bench, his guitar lying on his lap. When they were nearly out of sight, he got to his feet and followed them, shuffling along drunkenly, carrying his old guitar.

Buck Rawlins lived in a shack on the outskirts of town. He opened the door and saw Rosie, the waitress at the Acme Saloon, combing her hair in front of a mirror that hung on one of the walls.

"Where's my supper?" he growled.

"On the stove where it always is. What do you think you're doin' with that shotgun?"

"Mind yer goddamn business."

Rawlins laid the shotgun on the kitchen table, then went to the cupboard and took out a bottle of whiskey and a glass. He sat at the kitchen table and poured himself some whiskey, waiting for Rosie to serve him.

She walked to the stove and ladled out a bowl of beef stew, placing it before him, along with some bread and fresh butter.

He tore off a piece of bread and stuffed it into his mouth, chewing like an old bull. She looked at him and couldn't help smiling, because she considered him a big baby underneath his noise and bluster. He didn't treat her well, but she loved him anyway. He spooned some of the stew into his mouth.

"Like it?" she asked.

"It'll do."

He never complimented her cooking, but she knew he liked it because he always cleaned off his plate or bowl. She watched him eat, then took off her apron apron and hung it up.

"Got to go to work now, hon. Try to behave yourself tonight, okay? Stay out of trouble for a change."

He grunted, and she bent over, kissing his cheek, squeezing his shoulder. He smelled like tobacco and whiskey. She turned and walked to the door.

He listened to her leave, but didn't look at her. It was hard for him to tell her how much he cared about her, because he thought it'd make him appear weak, and Buck Rawlins didn't like to appear weak. But he knew he'd probably be lying in a gutter someplace, if it weren't for her. She kept him clean, well fed, and loved. He didn't dare tell her how much she meant to him, because in his experience the moment you started being nice to women, that's when they thought about leaving. He'd been through it before and didn't want to go through it again.

He finished the bowl of stew, went to the stove, and got another. *Rosie sure is a damned good cook.* He sat at the table again and continued to eat.

His thoughts turned to John Stone. He'd been wondering what to do about him, whether to let Casey kill him or not. Rawlins was at war with himself over Stone. One part of him wanted to see him get killed, and the other part thought he should do his duty and help Stone.

He finished the bowl of stew and reached for his bottle of whiskey, as if maybe he could find the solution there.

Two red lamps glowed on either side of the door to Miss Elsie's place, and light streamed out of the windows. The door opened and two men came out, their arms around each other's shoulders, singing a bawdy song. Stone watched them pass, then entered Miss Elsie's place.

It looked pretty much as he'd seen it the previous night, except it was full of men and women, and a man played a violin in the corner. The customers sat on sofas and chairs, and women in tight-waisted gowns, their faces covered with makeup, sat with them, talking, giggling, flirting, and sometimes fondling them. A couple ascended the stairs toward the rooms on the second floor, and another couple came down the stairs, a satisfied smile on the man's face.

Stone took off his hat and spotted Miss Elsie on the other side of the room. She wore a green dress and was sitting beside Howard Conway, the day desk clerk at the Olympia Hotel. Her eyes widened when she noticed Stone, and she patted Conway's knee, getting to her feet and walking toward Stone, her upper breasts were shaking with her every step.

"Heard you wanted to speak with me," Stone said.

She smiled and waved the fan in her hand. "Could you come to my office for a moment? Won't take but a minute."

He followed her down the hallway, and they came to a large room with a desk, a sofa, and several comfortable chairs.

"Have a seat," she said. "Can I offer you something to drink?"

"Whiskey."

She poured a glass of whiskey for him and one for herself. He sat on the sofa and she sat opposite him on a chair, handing him his glass. He heard a woman laugh in the hallway, and the faint strains of the violin came to his ears.

"I just wanted to thank you personally for what you did last night," Miss Elsie said to Stone. "I've decided to put you on my payroll. Ten dollars a week, to show my appreciation. I pay it to Rawlins and I might as well pay it to you too." She opened a drawer of the desk behind her, took out a metal box, opened it, and counted out some coins, placing them on the coffee table before him. "That's your first week."

Stone looked at the money. "I can't take that."

"You earned it." She smiled, and her teeth were small and white except for one on the bottom that was made of gold. "Consider it a supplemental payment."

"The city pays me my salary. I think it's against the law for me to take a bribe."

"This isn't a bribe."

"I think the law would consider it a bribe."

"There's no law here except you and me."

"*I'm* the law," he said.

"I know that, and I'm just giving you a little present. Nothing wrong with that, is there?"

"I think there is, to tell you the truth."

She leaned back in her chair and scratched her chin. "You're the strangest lawman I ever seen."

"I've never done this kind of work before in my life."

"You sure did a good job here last night. Buck Rawlins himself couldn't't've done better."

"Sheriff Rawlins is a good man. Don't underestimate him."

"If you think he's something now, you should've seen him twenty years ago."

"A lot of people in this town have a short memory when it comes to Sheriff Rawlins."

"It's sad what's happened to him," Miss Elsie said. "Too much drink is affecting his mind. The people in this town used to love him, but now they're getting fed up with him. You look like you'd make a good sheriff."

"Not interested." Stone unbuttoned his shirt pocket and took out the picture of Marie. "You ever see this woman?"

Miss Elsie took the picture and squinted at it. "Maybe and maybe not," she said. "So many people look alike. Pretty little thing, though."

"Think hard."

She shrugged and handed the picture back. "Can't say for sure. I run into a lot of pretty girls in my profession, as I'm sure you can understand. They come and they go. Do you think she might be in the same business I'm in?"

"I hope not."

She smiled. "You don't approve of my business?"

"I guess it's better than starving to death in the street."

"Who's the woman?"

"Friend of mine."

"If I think of anything, I'll let you know. You can show the picture to the other girls, if you like. Maybe one of them ran into her someplace along the way. My girls have been around. Sure you won't take the money?"

"I'm sure."

She put the money back into her metal box. "If there's ever anything else I can do for you, don't hesitate to ask. If you want to spend some time with one of my ladies, feel free to do so—on the house, of course. It'd be a pleasure to entertain you, Sheriff Stone."

"I don't think so, but thank you anyway, Miss Elsie."

She looked askance at him. "You're kind of a tightass, aren't you, John Stone?"

"Guess so, Miss Elsie." Then something occurred to him. "Say, you wouldn't have a room here for me, would you?"

"Where are you staying now?"

"With Mayor Randlett."

She thought for a few moments. "How do you like attics?"

"They're okay with me, if they're quiet."

"I could put a bed up there. There'd be a lot of room, and it'd be plenty quiet. When would you like to move in?"

"I could get my things right now and come back in a half hour or so."

"The bunk will be waiting for you. You can even take your meals in the kitchen with the rest of us, if you like."

Stone walked into the Randlett mansion, and Esmeralda came toward him out of the darkness.

"I'd like to talk with Mayor Randlett," he said.

"The mayor's out," Esmeralda replied.

"Is Miss Randlett in?"

"She's upstairs in her room."

"Do you think I could speak with her?"

"I'll ask her."

Esmeralda headed for the stairs, and Stone walked into the parlor, sitting on one of the chairs. Opposite him was the fireplace, and above it was a gigantic painting of a woman who looked something like Jennifer. Stone assumed it was Jennifer's mother.

Jennifer entered the living room, wearing the same dress she'd had on at dinner. "You wanted to see me, Captain Stone?" she asked with a smile.

Stone got to his feet. "Yes, I wanted to tell you that I'm moving out."

The smile disappeared. "Moving out?"

"Yes, I've found another place to live. You and your father have been very kind to me, but I thought I should have my own place. Didn't want to get in the way here."

"You weren't in the way."

"I thought it would be best this way."

"Where's your new place?"

Stone felt the color coming into his face, but she'd find out the truth sooner or later anyway.

"I've taken a room at the other end of town," he said.

"Whereabouts on the other end of town?"

He swallowed hard. "At Miss Elsie's place."

There was silence for a few moments, then she said, "I see."

He smiled nervously. "Well, thank you very much for everything. You and your father have been very kind." He realized he was talking too fast and too loud. "I'll go upstairs and get my things now."

He fled from the parlor, wondering what she must be thinking of him. She'd shown an expression of surprise or maybe even shock for a second, but then her face had regained its customary composure.

In his room upstairs, he stuffed his belongings into his saddlebags. He picked up his rifle, looked around to make sure he wasn't leaving anything, and spotted his razor lying next to the washbasin. Tossing it into the saddlebag, he left the room.

Jennifer was waiting for him at the bottom of the stairs. "I hope you'll be happy at Miss Elsie's," she said without a trace of sarcasm in her voice.

"It'll only be for a month," he replied, "and then I'm moving on. Thank you again for your hospitality. You and your father have been just wonderful, but sometimes a man likes to be on his own. I'm sure you understand. And now if you'll excuse me, I'd better get moving on. I've got a lot to do tonight."

He dashed toward the door, and Esmeralda held it open for him. The cool night air hit him in the face as he made his way to the street, his saddlebags slung over his shoulder and his rifle in his right hand.

Jennifer stood by the window and watched him go. *That's what men are like*, she said to herself. *They always take the easy way*.

She climbed the stairs to her bedroom, a troubled expression on her face. It bothered her to think that he was the only man who interested her, and he didn't care about her at all.

She entered her bedroom and pinched her lips together in frustration. On the dresser in front of her was the book she'd been reading when Esmeralda had come to tell her that John Stone wanted to speak with her.

In a sudden angry motion she picked up the book and was going to throw it across the room, but caught herself, took a deep breath, and sat down.

"Damn!" she muttered, opening the book to the page she'd been reading before. "Damn!"

6

THE LIGHTS OF Petie twinkled in the distance as Deke Casey and his men gathered on a hill west of town.

"We seen him and we know his routine pretty good," Casey told them, unfolding a map he'd drawn of Petie. "All we have to do is ride into town and shoot the son of a bitch." He pointed to the sheriff's office, and moonlight cast dark shadows over his unshaven face as he spoke. "He works out of this buildin' here and patrols the town back and forth, so he won't be hard to find. We'll just ride into town and track him down. When we find him, Schuler here'll face off with him."

"He didn't look like much to me," Schuler said contemptuously.

"We've all been around a long time," Casey told them, "and we know that sometimes things don't go the way we want. If Schuler don't git Stone, then the rest of us'll draw on him together, and we won't stop shootin' until he ain't movin' no more."

"I'll git him," Schuler said. "Don't you worry none about that."

"After Stone's dead," Casey continued, "we'll ride over to

the bank, blow down the doors, and take the money. Then we'll head south toward Mexico, and have us a good time with the señoritas. Any questions?"

Tom Hurley raised his hand. "It all sounds real good, but what if Rawlins horns in?"

Schuler spat into the dust beside him. "I'll kill him too."

Hurley grinned. "You're full of piss and vinegar tonight, ain't you?"

"You don't think I can handle him?"

Casey held up his hand. "Let's not argue, boys. Any other questions?"

Nobody raised his hand.

"We all know what we gotta do," Casey said. "From here on out, keep yer eyes open and be ready for anythin'."

Schuler quick-drew his pistol, and before anybody could blink it was pointing at them. "John Stone is as good as dead," he said. "You fellers just stay out of my way, understand?"

They nodded solemnly. Schuler stuffed his pistol back into his holster.

Casey climbed to his feet and walked toward the horses. His men followed, their pistols loaded, their gunbelts loaded with cartridges, and more cartridges were carried in their bulging pockets. They climbed onto their saddles and Casey led the way down the trail that led to Petie, glowing far away in the midst of the vast black prairie.

John Stone stood in Miss Elsie's backyard, his legs spread apart and his hat low over his eyes. He faced a row of bottles and cans propped on the fence twenty-five yards away, illuminated by light emanating from the rear windows of Miss Elsie's kitchen.

He tensed, then whipped out both his Colts and pulled the triggers. The night exploded as the cartridges fired, and on the fence in the distance the bottles were smashed apart and the tin cans went flying into the air. Stone, in his gunfighter's crouch, continued triggering his pistols until the bottles and cans were gone, and only a few shards of glass remained.

He holstered his Colts and turned back to the building. He'd been shooting bottles and cans for the past half hour and now his supply was depleted. Climbing the stairs, he entered the kitchen and saw Beatrice, Miss Elsie's cook, pull a tray of cookies out of the oven.

"Want one?" she asked.

She flipped one off the tray, and he caught it in his hand. Winking, chewing, he passed through a hallway and opened a door.

This was the part of the building where Miss Elsie lived with Beatrice. It also contained storerooms for food, liquor, sheets, and blankets. He passed a stack of old newspapers, and then the light became feeble as he ascended the final flight of stairs to the attic. Stepping carefully, he came to the attic door and flung it open. A musty fragrance came to him, and he lit a match, touching it to the wick of the lamp on the dresser nearby.

The attic became bathed in the golden glow of the lamp, and Stone saw stacks of suitcases and old trunks jumbled together against a wall. Gowns, coats, and wraps hung from pegs on the walls, or overflowed out of boxes and crates, a profusion of gay colors and fabrics that once had graced the figures of beautiful ladies, and now were growing moldy and moth-eaten, forgotten vestiges of wild nights filled with laughter, whiskey, and naughtiness.

Chairs, tables, sofas, and beds with broken legs or cracked surfaces were stacked everywhere, and cheap old jewelry glittered faintly in boxes and baskets. Stone carried his lamp toward a wide brass bed set up at the far end of the attic next to a window that overlooked the backyard.

Stone placed the lamp on the dresser. He opened a drawer and pulled out a box of ammunition, reloading his pistols and pushing fresh cartridges into the slots in his gunbelts. Across the room, he could see his reflection in an old yellowing mirror, a tall figure with his face hidden by the shadow cast by his wide-brimmed cavalry hat.

It was time to go to work. He walked out of the attic and climbed down the stairs to the kitchen, where Beatrice was preparing a haunch of beef for the oven.

"You hungry?" she asked.

"A little."

"Have a seat."

Stone took off his hat and sat at the long table where the girls usually dined together, but now they were working in the front of the house, entertaining men. Beatrice was a hefty middle-aged woman wearing an apron and a long dress. She placed half a cold chicken in front of Stone, along with a bowl of potato salad and a loaf of bread. Then she brought him a pot of coffee and a cup.

He picked up the chicken in his hands and tore a chunk off it with his teeth, glad that he didn't have to mind his manners, as in the Randlett home. If his mother had seen him eat with his hands, she'd smack him across his face, but times had changed and good table manners didn't account for much on the frontier.

"How do you like yer room?" Beatrice asked, sprinkling the haunch of meat before her with salt.

"I like it fine."

"A few of the girls have kinda mentioned to me that they wouldn't mind keepin' you company up there, if you're interested."

"Tell them I'm engaged to git married."

The door opened and a young blond woman entered, wearing a pink dress with a low bodice. "I need some coffee," she said, and then noticed Stone. "Well, look who's here—our deputy sheriff."

"That's Veronica," Beatrice said.

Veronica poured herself a cup of coffee and sat opposite Stone. She had long blond hair and so much makeup on her face she looked like a painted doll. "How do you like living in a whorehouse?" she asked.

"Can't beat the food."

"We're famous for a lot of things here, but food ain't one of them. Maybe you ought to try some of our other attractions."

"Where you from, Veronica?"

"Mississippi."

Stone took out the picture of Marie and showed it to her. "Ever see this woman?"

"This the one you're supposed to be gittin' married to, only nobody knows where she is?" Veronica wrinkled her brow as she looked at the picture. "She's real purty, but I don't think I ever seen her."

Stone returned the picture to his shirt pocket. Veronica sipped her coffee. "God, I'm ready to go to sleep and the night ain't even started yet. The house is full of crazy cowboys and I'm afraid they're just gonna wear my poor old body out."

The door to the kitchen opened and Miss Elsie walked in. "Get out in the parlor," she said to Veronica. "It's full of customers."

Veronica frowned as she lifted her cup of coffee and moved toward the door.

"See you later, Deputy Stone," she said. "Be careful where you put yer gun tonight, hear?"

Miss Elsie picked a cookie out of the bowl. "My girls have been in a tizzy ever since you moved in here, Deputy Stone. One of them's liable to ambush you in the middle of the night when you're on your way to the attic. What're you going to do then, John Stone? Show her the picture of the girl you're supposed to marry?"

"I'm sure your girls have better manners than to attack a man in the dark unawares."

"I wouldn't bet on that if I were you."

Sheriff Rawlins sat on his bed, drinking a glass of whiskey. Rosie had gone to work, and he was alone. A lamp on the night-table next to the bed cast a wan light on his mustache and deeply lined face. He still was wondering what to do about John Stone.

He was pretty certain that Deke Casey and his men would try to kill John Stone that night. One part of him thought he should save John Stone's life, and the other part said he should let John Stone die.

He was leaning toward the latter position, because he didn't like John Stone one bit. If Stone thought he was good enough to be a lawman, let him take a lawman's chances. It'd be a good thing for the people of Petie to see John Stone die. They'd realize he wasn't the great hero that they'd imagined.

Rawlins thought it was sickening the way everybody in town was playing up to John Stone. Even Rosie spoke of him as if he was something special, and he was nothing more than another saddle bum who happened to get lucky one day. Women were wild about Stone, the way they'd been wild about him in the old days. Rawlins touched a hand to his stomach. He

was getting a paunch, and didn't like it. His face looked like
a road map. He had a few gray hairs on his head. And John
Stone was in the prime of youth, flat-stomached, clear-eyed,
and strong. Rawlins grit his teeth in frustration. Everybody
loved John Stone, and everybody was embarrassed by Buck
Rawlins.

I'll let them kill him, he thought. He raised his glass of whiskey to his lips and drank. *Let him take care of his own ass, if
he thinks he's so goddamned smart*. He lit a stogie, pulled off
his boots, and lay flat on the bed, a smile on his face. He'd
made his decision and now he could relax. Maybe he could
even fall asleep. Later on they'd come and tell him some men
had shot John Stone, and he'd go out and see Stone bleeding
in the middle of a street somewheres. That'd be the end of a
man who'd thought he was better than he really was.

Rawlins's head was propped up by the pillow, and he puffed
his stogie calmly. Facing him was a portrait of Bobby Lee
hanging on the wall. The wick of the lamp flickered, making
the features of Bobby Lee's face move, as if he were alive.
Bobby Lee seemed to be looking at Rawlins reproachfully, as
if he disapproved of what Rawlins was doing. Bobby Lee shook
his head and pursed his lips.

Rawlins recalled the rumors he'd heard about John Stone's
service in the war. Stone had fought in the cavalry under Jeb
Stuart and had come out a captain. They said he'd seen a lot
of action.

Rawlins had been in the war too, and also had been in many
battles. From Georgia originally, he'd deeply believed in the
Southern cause. He already was Sheriff of Petie when the war
broke out, but he quit and went east to sign up, fighting Yankees
for four long years. Then, when the war was over, he made
his way back to Petie, and they'd gladly given him his old job
back. A detachment of Confederate infantry had been stationed
near the town during the war, and they'd provided protection,
but they'd been gone for some time and the town was having
problems with rowdies and gunfighters again. Rawlins quickly
asserted himself and restored law and order.

But it wasn't the same, because the war had embittered him.
He began drinking more than usual to forget the horrors of
frontline combat, and he had contempt for the men of the town

who'd never gone to war. He considered them slackers and cowards and hated their guts, and never bothered to hide his feelings about them. They in turn became increasingly disenchanted with him, and his relations with the townspeople had been deteriorating steadily ever since he returned.

But John Stone hadn't been a slacker or a coward, Rawlins had to admit to himself. Stone had fought for Bobby Lee and the Confederacy too, and they'd all gone down to crushing defeat at the hands of the Yankees.

Rawlins still got angry when he thought about the war. He'd loved the Old South, and now it was gone forever. He remembered Jeb Stuart, who'd been one of his heroes. He'd actually seen Jeb Stuart at Chancellorsville. Jeb Stuart had come to Stonewall Jackson's headquarters, wearing his great plumed hat, and Rawlins had been in the vicinity. He'd cheered Jeb Stuart along with the rest of the men, and later Jeb Stuart's cavalry had provided the screen for a roundabout twelve-mile march to the front by Stonewall Jackson's artillery and infantry, of which Rawlins had been a member. That'd been in '63, when Rawlins had been a sergeant, and they'd hit Joe Hooker's right flank hard.

Rawlins remembered how he and the rest of Stonewall Jackson's men charged through the woods on a two-mile-wide front, three divisions deep, screaming at the tops of their lungs, and the Yankees ran for their lives. Rawlins realized he and Stone evidently had been there at the same time.

He remembered how the battlefield had been covered with bodies afterward. The Yankees lost seventeen thousand men, and the Confederacy lost thirteen thousand in five days of fighting. Stonewall Jackson had been wounded, and died eight days later, but Chancellorsville had been a great victory for the Confederacy, and John Stone had been there.

In fact, during the shifting tides of battle, Jeb Stuart had taken command of Rawlins's unit for a while, and they'd faced a Yankee force that outnumbered them three to one. It had been a bloodbath, but the Yankees, under John Sedgwick, finally retreated across the Rappahannock during the night, and the battle was substantially over.

Rawlins sat up in bed. He realized that Stone and he had served in the same sector, under the same commander, fighting the same fight! He recalled seeing Confederate cavalrymen charge John Sedgwick's position, and John Stone might've been one of those cavalrymen. Since Stone had been an officer, he would've been in front leading the way. Rawlins recalled how brave those cavalry officers had been, and how dangerous it was to be in front of a cavalry charge, an easy target for Yankee sharpshooters.

In the confusion of battle, infantry and cavalry sometime had gotten intermingled. Rawlins realized he and Stone might've been in sight of each other during the fight, perhaps actually had even seen each other, although they didn't know it.

Rawlins puffed his stogie nervously. The terror and thrill of the war came back to him. He recalled the charges and retreats, the hand-to-hand struggles with the Yankees, the explosions of artillery, his company commander shot in the head, and old Jeb Stuart urging them onward to the victory that was finally theirs.

John Stone was there, Rawlins said to himself. He realized that he and Stone had been members of the brotherhood that fought shoulder to shoulder against the Yankees at Chancellorsville, and at least that time they'd prevailed. Rawlins and the other soldiers on the Confederate side had felt like great warriors, and now, sitting on his bed, Rawlins remembered how wonderful the taste of victory had been.

Stone had been there. Rawlins chewed on his stogie and frowned. He swung his feet to the floor and pulled on his boots. Strapping on his gunbelt, he reached for his shotgun, cracking it open and loading both barrels.

He didn't like Stone much, but knew what he had to do. They'd fought together at Chancellorsville under Jeb Stuart and Bobby Lee, and by Christ they'd fight together again.

In a column of twos, the remaining members of the Deke Casey gang rode into Petie. They looked like a group of cowboys coming to have a good time, and nobody paid any special attention to them. Light from windows of saloons, restaurants, and private homes illuminated their faces as they passed the Petie Savings Bank, and they gazed at it with desire in their eyes. They knew it was full of money, and soon it'd all be theirs.

Casey rode in front, with Schuler beside him. Schuler held

his reins with one hand while resting the palm of his other hand on his thigh, sitting tall in his saddle, excited about the gunfight that lay ahead.

He had complete confidence in himself. Maybe the most famous gunfighters of the frontier were faster than he, but not John Stone, a two-bit deputy sheriff that nobody ever had heard of before.

Ahead was the Paradise Saloon, its bright light spilling onto groups of men having conversations on the sidewalk and in the street. The sound of the saloon's piano could be heard clearly. Casey angled his head toward the Paradise, and his men followed him to the hitching rail. They dismounted, tied up their horses, and hitched up their gunbelts.

Casey turned to Schuler. "You ready?"

Schuler nodded, a cocky smile on his face. He climbed onto the boardwalk and advanced toward the doors of the Paradise Saloon. The others followed him, and Schuler pushed a drunk out of his way. The drunk went flying into a wall, striking it with his face. Schuler threw open the doors to the Paradise Saloon and stepped inside. His skin tingled with excitement and he wiggled his fingers, keeping them limber. Scanning back and forth through the thick smoke, he saw the Paradise full of men, but John Stone was nowhere in sight.

"I don't see him," Schuler said to Casey. "Lemme take a better look. He might be hidin' behind somebody."

Casey and the rest of his men stood by the door as Schuler made his way toward the bar. Schuler felt alert and intensely alive, ready to gunfight. He wished John Stone would appear in front of him, so he could gun him down.

Schuler reached the bar and leaned back against it, scrutinizing the people in front of him once more. Stone wasn't sitting at the tables or standing at the bar.

"What's your pleasure?" asked the bartender.

"I'm lookin' for John Stone," Schuler replied. "Know where he's at?"

"Ain't seen him all night."

Schuler returned to Casey and the others standing beside the door.

"He ain't here."

"I can see that," Casey said dryly. "Let's check the Acme."

They turned around and walked out of the Paradise, crossing the street, heading for the Acme Saloon. Casey led the others, with Schuler beside him, wiggling his fingers, working his shoulders, trying to stay loose.

I'm ready, Schuler said to himself. *Where the hell is he?*

John Stone walked down the middle of the street at the other end of town. It was dark and peaceful, and no stores or other businesses were open. He hoped it'd be an easy night.

Angling toward the sidewalk, he checked a few doors to make sure they were locked. He looked into alleys and glanced up at rooftops. He didn't think he'd ever walk through a town again without checking the rooftops.

Approaching another alley, he stopped and looked into it. A dark form lay there snoring. Stone walked into the alley and dropped to one knee. Before him lay an old geezer with a gray beard, wearing a ruined narrow-brimmed hat, snoring away. Stone decided he'd better lock him in jail and let him sleep it off, otherwise somebody was liable to rob him in the alley.

Stone lifted the old geezer and threw him over his shoulder, and the old geezer grumbled something, then continued to snore as if nothing had happened. The strong odor of fermented spirits came over Stone, and he coughed as he walked out of the alley. He crossed the street and headed toward the sheriff's office.

The sound of an out-of-tune guitar came to him. Stone saw a figure on a bench straight ahead, strumming lightly. It was Toby Muldoon, who looked up as Stone approached.

"What you got there, Cap'n."

"Somebody who needs a place to sleep. What're you doing out here all by yourself?"

"Just playin' me old guitar. Buy me a drink?"

Stone tossed him a few coins. Toby reached out and caught them in midair. "Watch yer step, Cap'n. You never know who you're liable to run into on a dark night."

Stone continued on his way to the sheriff's office. He unlocked it, glancing at the reflection in the glass of the roof across the street, but this time there was no head showing at the peak.

He entered the office, unlocked the jail area, and dropped

the drunk onto a cot. Then he returned to the main office and
lit a lamp. There were no instructions for him. Rawlins was
ignoring him as usual, but he didn't care. In another few weeks
Stone would be long gone and Rawlins could have Petie all to
himself.

Stone sat at Pritchard's desk and rolled himself a cigarette.
He blew smoke into the air, took out his pistols, spun the cyl-
inders, and dropped them back into their holsters.

Now what? He wished he had a book or a newspaper, but
there was nothing to read except official correspondence and
that didn't interest him. Tomorrow he'd have to see about find-
ing some reading material. He thought maybe the girls at Miss
Elsie's had books, those who could read, although their taste
probably would be different from his. He'd be willing to settle
for a recent newspaper, to find out what was going on in the
world.

He leaned back in the chair and placed his boots on the desk.
After I finish this cigarette, I think I'll check the saloons.

Fritz Schuler stepped onto the sidewalk in front of the Acme
Saloon and moved toward the doors. He was aware that the
other members of the gang were watching him, relying upon
him to outdraw John Stone, and that made him feel important.
He liked to feel important, and hoped someday to take over the
gang from Casey, who was getting old and tired, and wasn't
so fast with a gun.

Schuler pushed the doors open and stepped inside the Acme,
which was smaller than the Paradise, and the waitresses were
said to be prettier. Schuler would like to shoot Stone in front
of pretty waitresses, so he could impress them with his shooting skill. He wanted to see the horror on their faces, and then
their admiration when they realized he was a great gunfighter.
Maybe someday, if he kept on the way he was going, he could
become famous, and even newspapers in the East would show
his picture and tell the story of his courage and fast hand.

He scanned the Acme from side to side, looking for John
Stone, but the tall man wasn't there. His shoulders went limp
and his fingers felt like putty. He'd been keyed up for the fight,
but now the tension was leaving him and he felt perturbed.
Where the hell is the son of a bitch?

"Looks like he ain't here," Casey said.

"How's about a drink?" asked Hind, the shortest member of the gang, only five feet four. His shirt, pants, and hat were all too big for him, and he looked comical, but he had the soul of a killer and there was nothing funny about him.

"Might as well," Casey said. "What the hell."

They walked toward the bar, Schuler leading the way. Schuler pushed a cowboy to the side, because he was feeling mean and looking for trouble. The cowboy caught his balance and said, "Hey!"

Schuler turned and faced him, his legs spread apart and his fingers hanging loose. "You got somethin' to say to me?" he asked the cowboy.

The cowboy looked at Schuler, saw his tied-down holster and his gunfighter's stance, and decided he wasn't ready to push it to the limit.

"Nothin'," said the cowboy.

"It'd damn well better be nothin', otherwise I'll blow yer fuckin' head off."

The cowboy sulked off into the darkness, and the Deke Casey gang moved toward the bar. Men got out of their way; the citizens of Petie generally tried to avoid trouble. Schuler pounded the heel of his fist on the bar. "Whiskey!"

The bartender came running with glasses and a bottle, setting them up before Schuler and the others. Schuler poured two fingers of whiskey into his glass and passed the bottle to Deke Casey, then Schuler looked into the glass and saw the reflection of light against the surface of the amber liquid. The light danced and jiggled, and Schuler wished John Stone would walk into the Acme at that moment, so he could gun him down before the large audience that was assembled there.

Casey raised his glass in the air. "To Bloody Bill," he said.

The members of the gang drained their glasses. Schuler turned around and saw a waitress passing by, carrying a tray covered with empty glasses. Schuler reached out and grabbed her arm, upsetting her balance, and the glasses went crashing to the floor.

"What's yer hurry?" Schuler asked.

"Git yer hand off'n me!" the waitress replied, a young brunette with freckles on her face, struggling and squirming.

Schuler laughed, pulled her toward him, and kissed her lips, then pushed her away.

She wiped her mouth with the back of her hand and glowered at him. Schuler hoped someone would step forward to defend the waitress's honor, but no one moved. A little old man with a broom, wearing a stained apron, came to sweep up the broken glass. The waitress stepped back into the crowd. The atmosphere in the Acme had become tense, and some men drained their glasses, heading for the door.

"Where's that son of a bitch, John Stone!" Schuler shouted. His voice echoed across the Acme, and no one answered him. Schuler spit on the floor and looked at Casey. "Should we wait for him here, or go out lookin' for him?"

"Let's go to his office. That's probably where he is."

Schuler felt himself getting angry. He was ready to fight but there was no one to fight with. Walking toward the door, he lashed out with his foot and kicked a table over onto the two men sitting at it, and the men raised their hands to their faces to protect themselves.

"I never seen such a yeller bunch of bastards in my life," Schuler growled as he walked toward the door.

He stepped onto the sidewalk, and the other members of the gang coalesced around him. Grim-faced, they marched down the street toward the sheriff's office.

Stone threw his cigarette butt into the cuspidor, where it hissed and went out. He stood, readjusted his gunbelt, and walked toward the door. He thought he'd get a drink and check out the town.

He locked the office and headed toward the Acme, his footsteps sounding on the planks of the boardwalk. A few drunks lolled on benches in front of stores, but the real action was up the street, where he could see the bright lights of the saloons and hear the plinking of pianos.

He saw a group of men moving toward him on the sidewalk. There wouldn't be room for all of them on the narrow passage between buildings and hitching rails, so Stone jumped down to the dirt and veered toward the center of the street.

The men coming toward him turned and hopped into the street also. Stone thought they were going to cross, but instead they advanced up the middle, heading straight for him. There were six of them, led by a young man with long blond sideburns. Stone moved toward the sidewalk to let them pass.

"Where you runnin' to, Stone?" asked Fritz Schuler.

Stone stopped in the middle of the dark street. "I'm not running anywhere."

Schuler walked determinedly toward Stone, feeling the euphoria that preceded a gunfight. "I been lookin' for you," he told Stone.

"What for?"

The other members of the gang split up, Casey, Hurley, and Cotler moving to Stone's right, and Ramsay and Hind moving toward Stone's left. Stone saw the coalition form in front of him, and it didn't look good.

"They tell me you're a coward," Schuler said, his arms held away from his body, wiggling his fingers.

Stone stiffened his spine and moved his legs apart. The two men faced each other in the middle of the street, staring into each other's eyes for several seconds, then Schuler stepped forward, his spurs jangling each time his feet touched the ground. Schuler came to a halt about fifteen yards in front of Stone, and the other members of the gang advanced too, moving closer to Stone on both sides of the street.

The crowd in front of the saloons saw the confrontation and heard the words that had passed between Stone and Schuler. They moved cautiously down the sidewalks on both sides of the street, to watch what was going to happen. Schuler hoped some ladies were there, to see him in action.

"So you're John Stone," Schuler said. "They tell me you're a big hero around here."

The two men looked at each other, still as statues, their hands hanging in the air, fingers loose, ready to reach for their guns. Not far away, Deke Casey winked at the rest of his men, signaling them to get ready, and they moved their hands toward their guns. On the sidewalks, the townspeople watched eagerly, their eyes glittering with excitement.

Schuler smiled. Everybody was looking at him, waiting for him to reach for his guns. John Stone stood solidly in the wan light, a big target, and Schuler didn't think he could miss.

Stone watched him carefully, alert but not tense, wondering whether he should draw first or let his adversary make the move. He couldn't help wondering why this man, whom he'd never seen before in his life, wanted to kill him.

The smile vanished from Schuler's face, and his right hand dived toward his gun, but Stone's two Colts were already clearing their holsters. Stone held both Colts in front of him and triggered. His gunshots reverberated across the town as Schuler was pulling his pistol out of its holster. Schuler's last thought was *he's too fast* and then both bullets struck him in the chest simultaneously like two sledgehammers, knocking him off his feet. He felt himself falling through space, and spit blood as he pulled his trigger involuntarily. His gun fired wildly, and the bullet flew across the street, hitting a bystander in the shin-bone.

Schuler fell into a clump on the ground, and Stone arose from his crouch, both gun barrels smoking.

"Get him!" hollered Deke Casey.

Casey yanked out his pistol, and a split second later heard the loudest explosion of his life, but he didn't hear it for long. Sheriff Buck Rawlins was behind him, his sawed-off shotgun in his hands, and he blew Casey's head to smithereens. Casey's blood and brains sprayed through the air, and Rawlins pivoted, firing the other barrel into the guts of Tom Hurley, the outlaw with the ratlike face. Hurley went flying backward, and Rawlins charged the third outlaw near him, Cotler, and slammed him in the face with the butt of his shotgun.

Meanwhile, Stone saw two men to his left reaching for their guns. He swung his Colts around and shot a barrage into the stomach of Fred Ramsay, but the last outlaw, Hind, the smallest of the bunch, had drawn a bead on Stone and was squeezing his trigger.

Suddenly, out of the shadows, a cracked violin with a string missing swung down and whacked Hind on the top of his head. Hind's pistol fired, and Stone felt something hot and terrible punch into his shoulder. Holding steady, he fired both his Colts at Hind, and the impact of the bullets spun Hind around, blood spiraling through the air, as Hind tumbled toward the ground.

All the action had taken only a few seconds. Stone scanned the scene in front of him, holding his pistols ready to fire, but no one else was moving on him. He grit his teeth in pain, and then couldn't hold up his left arm anymore. It dropped to his side, and his left hand went numb. His fingers lost their ability to grip, and one of his Colts fell to the ground.

He looked at Sheriff Rawlins and Toby Muldoon, the latter smiling broadly, holding his broken guitar in his right hand. The bodies of six men were on the ground in the middle of the street. The crowd of onlookers crept out of the alleys where they'd fled for shelter when the shooting started.

"Is it all over?" one of them asked fearfully.

"Yeah," replied Rawlins, "this horseshit usually don't take long." He looked at Stone and shook his head in derision. "You damn fool—you walked right into them!"

Stone's blood was soaking into his shirt, and he felt light-headed. "I didn't know they wanted to kill me."

Rawlins pointed at the body lying nearly headless in the middle of the street. "That's Deke Casey!"

"Who's Deke Casey?"

"One of the most wanted men on the frontier, and you didn't know who in hell he was?"

"Never heard of him before."

Rawlins snorted. "Some deputy sheriff you are. I thought you was supposed to be smart." He took a few steps toward Stone and saw the widening stain on his shirt. "Looks like you need the doc."

"I'll be okay," Stone said, but he was reeling from side to side, blinking his eyes, trying to hold on.

"I'll git the doc," Muldoon said, running away, still holding onto his broken guitar.

Stone felt the black waves pass over him, but he didn't want to let go. He took a step toward Sheriff Rawlins. "I guess you saved my life, Sheriff. I want to thank you."

He held out his hand, to shake with Rawlins, but Rawlins sneered and took a step backward. "I was just doin' my job," Rawlins said. "You couldn't handle it yerself, so's I had to help you out."

"Got to sit down," Stone said weakly.

He took a step toward the sidewalk, stumbled, and fell to the ground. The big black waves swept over him, engulfed him, and carried him away.

7

RISING UP OUT of the dark clouds, John Stone became aware of intense fiery pain in his shoulder from his neck down to his bicep. He opened his eyes slowly, and the attic of Miss Elsie's place came into focus. Crinoline and old moldy gowns hung over a mirror on the dresser beyond the foot of the bed, and he smelled perfume.

"I think he's come to," said a female voice.

Stone turned his head to the side, and saw Dorothy Brenner, the brunette woman he's saved from the beating by the drunken cowboy, and Veronica, the blonde. They were seated on chairs, and Dorothy was knitting something, while Veronica did crochet work.

"How do you feel?" Veronica asked, leaning over him. She wore a low-cut dress, and he could see the tops of her breasts.

"It hurts," he replied, and his voice came out like the croak of a frog. "What day is it?"

"Friday."

Stone closed his eyes and tried to think. He remembered that he'd been shot on Wednesday night. That meant he'd been unconscious for about a day and a half.

"Can I get you anything?" Dorothy Brenner asked.

Stone took stock of himself. He didn't feel hungry, but could use a drink. "Got any whiskey?"

"Just happen to have a bottle right here," Dorothy replied.

She poured him a half glass and brought it to his lips. He took a sip, and it helped the pain go away.

"How's about a cigarette?" he asked.

"Don't you think you should eat something?"

"I'm not hungry."

"I'll give you a cigarette if you promise to eat something."

Veronica rolled the cigarette, and Stone remembered the gun-fight on Wednesday night. If it hadn't been for Rawlins and Toby Muldoon, he would've been killed. The gunmen had outnumbered him six to one, and he's just blundered into them. It had been another brush with death, and he'd been lucky. Maybe next time he wouldn't be so lucky.

Veronica lit the cigarette and handed it to Stone. He accepted it and took a drag, the smoke making his head spin.

Dorothy Brenner arose from her chair. "I'll go down and get you something to eat."

She walked toward the stairs, leaving Stone alone with Veronica, who reached forward and brushed cigarette ashes off the sheet.

"Anything happen in town while I've been lying here?" he asked.

"It's been quiet. Doc McGrath has been up to see you a few times. He says you're comin' along just fine."

"Has Sheriff Rawlins been by?"

"Nope."

Stone puffed his cigarette and thought about Rawlins. He knew Rawlins didn't like him, but Rawlins had saved his life anyway. Stone had tried to thank Rawlins after the shooting, but the sheriff wouldn't accept his gratitude, and instead insulted him. What a strange man Rawlins was.

Dorothy Brenner returned to the attic, carrying a tray that she placed on Stone's lap.

"You've got to eat it all," she said.

He looked down at a thick steak, some vegetables, a cup of coffee, and a wedge of apple pie. The aroma rose to his nostrils, provoking his appetite.

"I'll cut up yer steak for you," Veronica said.

She leaned over him and picked up the knife and fork, slicing into the meat, her face only inches from his and her perfume enveloping him.

"Later on in the day I'll give you a shave," she said. "I used to shave my daddy all the time, and he said I was real good at it."

Stone placed some steak into his mouth. It was tender and juicy, and he hoped it would replenish his strength quickly. He didn't like to be helpless, laid up in bed like an old man. He figured he should be back on the job in about a week.

"Where'd you learn to be so fast with a gun?" Dorothy asked him.

"Practice," he replied.

"I guess you don't know who you outgunned."

Stone remembered the man with the long blond sideburns and pinkish complexion. "Never saw him before."

"His name was Fritz Schuler, and he had a reputation for bein' real fast, but I guess you was faster. He was a wanted man, and so was the rest of them. They was the Deke Casey gang."

Stone recalled Sheriff Rawlins telling him about Casey on the night of the shooting, but the name hadn't meant anything to him then and still didn't.

"Rawlins said it was part of the same gang that come to rob the bank last week," Dorothy continued. "He says they was here to pay you back for killin' their owlhoot pardners, and then they was gonna rob the bank again. He found dynamite in their saddlebags, and he figgers they was just gonna blow down the bank door and take whatever they wanted. He said that feller who tried to bushwhack you the other night was prob'ly in the Deke Casey gang too."

Stone speared a roast potato with his fork. Now it all made sense. Rawlins was an old lawman and he'd put the pieces together, but Stone, who didn't know anything about being a lawman, had just been wandering around like a fool, unable to figure out what was going on.

"Rawlins is a good man," Stone said. "I don't think this town appreciates him."

"That's because he's drunk all the time, and he pushes people around."

"This town'd be in bad shape without him."

"We're in bad shape with him, but I guess he's better than nothin'. A lot of people think you should take over his job and become sheriff here."

"I don't know a damn thing about it. If it hadn't been for Rawlins, I'd be dead right now. When my time is up here, I'm moving on."

"Personally," said Veronica, "I think you ought to be a fancy man."

Dorothy Brenner nodded. "That's what I think too."

John Stone pictured himself in a tight suit and ruffled shirt, wearing a top hat, living off the earnings of girls like Veronica and Dorothy. "It's not me," he said.

"Not much to do," Veronica said. "Just lay on yer ass and be taken care of by wimmin, like now. Don't you like that?"

"Wouldn't want to make a career out of it."

"Why not?"

"If I had my choice, I'd like to have my own ranch."

"If you was a fancy man and saved yer money, you could end up with yer own ranch."

"I can't be a fancy man. I'm engaged to get married."

"But you don't even know where the girl you're gonna marry is."

"I'll find her."

"What if you don't?"

"Maybe I'll take your advice," Stone said with a smile. "Could I be your fancy man, Veronica?"

"Both of us could do a hell of a lot worse, John Stone."

Jennifer Randlett walked up the path that led to Miss Elsie's place. She wore a simple cotton dress, carried a large bouquet of flowers, and was nervous, not sure she was doing the right thing, but it was too late to turn back now. Her father would be shocked if he knew where she was headed.

She knocked on the front door between two red lamps. Several seconds passed, during which she pinched her lips together and tried to be steady, and then the door was opened by a young woman wearing bright red lipstick and heavily rouged cheeks.

"We're not hirin' anybody just now," said the woman, whose

name was Daisy. "Come back in a few weeks and we might have somethin' for you."

"I'm not applying for work," Jennifer replied. "I'm here to see John Stone."

Daisy didn't know whether to invite the visitor inside or not. She'd only been in town a few days and wasn't aware that she was dealing with the mayor's daughter.

"I think you'd better wait right here," Daisy said. "I'll get Miss Elsie."

Daisy walked away, and Jennifer gazed into the gaudy vestibule. The wallpaper was red and the lamps on the wall were burnished brass. She'd heard wild rumors about Miss Elsie's, and it had become a palace of sin in her mind, titillating and terrible. Jennifer realized Daisy hadn't been any older than she, and yet was a prostitute, paid to entertain men. Jennifer thought it must be awful to have to earn a living by letting drunken dirty cowboys crawl all over you every night.

Miss Elsie advanced across the vestibule, and Jennifer knew who she was; Miss Elsie had business with her father on several occasions.

"Good afternoon, Miss Randlett," Miss Elsie said, fluttering her Chinese fan. "Sorry to keep you waiting. Won't you come in? You say you'd like to see Captain Stone?"

Miss Elsie was bedecked with jewels, wearing an expensive gown, her curly blond hair carefully coiffed. Jennifer followed her into the parlor, where a few men were sitting around with some of the girls. One of the men was drunk, and he pointed unsteadily at Jennifer.

"I want that one!"

Miss Elsie led Jennifer to the kitchen. "I imagine this is a strange experience for you, visiting here. It must've taken a lot of courage. I guess you're quite fond of our deputy sheriff."

"He's a friend of the family," Jennifer said coolly. "If Sheriff Rawlins had been shot, I'd visit him also."

Miss Elsie smiled as if she didn't believe Jennifer, but Jennifer had learned that the mayor's daughter had to be calm in all situations and never let any emotions show.

"He's right up these stairs in the attic," Miss Elsie told her. "Two of the girls are looking after him. They're taking turns, because they all want to be with him. He certainly has a certain attraction for women, wouldn't you say?"

"As I told you, he's a friend of the family."

Jennifer had the impression that Miss Elsie was going to laugh in her face. *Is it that obvious?* Jennifer asked herself.

"I'm not going up with you," Miss Elsie said. "When you get old, you don't like to climb stairs. Would you like a vase for those flowers? Beatrice, get a vase for Miss Randlett."

Beatrice came away from the stove and took down a vase from a cupboard, putting the flowers into it.

"Give Deputy Stone a kiss for me," Beatrice said to Jennifer.

Jennifer carried the vase up the stairs to the attic, wondering how John Stone could prefer this to her mansion. The attic smelled like old clothes and faded perfume, and she walked past the worn trunks and hats of bygone eras to the bed near the window.

Veronica heard her approach and arose from her chair. "Do you see what I see?" she said to Dorothy Brenner.

"Looks like the mayor's daughter." Dorothy turned to Stone. "You've got company."

Stone looked at Jennifer moving toward him, carrying the vase full of flowers, and realized it was extremely unusual for a woman of her social standing to visit Miss Elsie's place. He was so surprised that he didn't know what to say.

Jennifer moved toward the side of his bed. "I brought you some flowers," she said, placing them on the table near his bed. "Hope you like them. I picked them myself in our garden."

Jennifer looked around, but couldn't see any chairs other than the ones Veronica and Dorothy Brenner had been sitting on.

"Take mine," Veronica said. "I'll get another."

"No, that's all right."

"Take it and stop being so damned prissy."

Veronica walked off into the far shadows of the endless attic, and Jennifer sat uncertainly in the chair. Nobody had ever talked to her like that before and she wasn't sure of how to handle it. She decided to make believe it hadn't happened, and turned to Stone with a smile.

"We were all very worried about you," she said.

"Nothing to worry about," he replied. "I'm doing all right."

"You look kind of pale."

"He lost a lot of blood," Dorothy Brenner said.

"Do you feel weak?" Jennifer asked.

"A little."

"Have you eaten?"

"Yes."

"Is there anything I could do?"

Veronica returned with a chair, and she heard Jennifer's question. "What could *you* do?" Veronica asked sarcastically.

"Anything *you* could do," Jennifer replied.

"I wouldn't be so sure of that, honey child," Veronica said, dropping onto the chair and crossing her legs.

Jennifer returned her attention to Stone. The sheet had dropped from his shoulders and she could see the dark blond hair on his chest. His left shoulder wore a massive bandage.

He was staring at the blossoms Jennifer had brought him, remembering the vast flower gardens planted around Albemarle. Many times Stone had walked with Marie in the gardens, hand in hand, opening their hearts to each other as birds sang around them and the sun shone brightly overhead. It had been paradise, and they thought they'd have that garden to walk in forever, but then the war came and that was the end of everything.

"Are you all right?" Jennifer asked softly.

Stone opened his eyes. "Just faded out," he said. "Sorry."

"I don't think you're looking well at all." She noticed the ashtray and glass of whiskey on the table. "Are you sure you're being cared for properly here?"

Veronica sniffed. "Don't worry, honey. We'll give him anything he needs."

Jennifer turned to her. "I'm just concerned that you might give him something he doesn't want."

Stone raised his hand. "Ladies. Please."

Jennifer smiled. "I think I'd better be going," she said. "Just thought I'd drop in to see you, Captain Stone. If there's anything I or my father can do for you, please don't hesitate to contact us."

Stone thanked her for her visit. She squeezed his hand, then turned around and walked across the attic. Stone heard her descending the stairs to the floor below.

"What a little bitch," Veronica said, placing her hands on her hips, making a funny face that was supposed to resemble Jennifer. "She ever talks to me like that again, I'll pull her tongue out by the roots."

"I feel kind of tired," Stone said. "I'm think I'm going to sleep for a while."

He closed his eyes and took a deep breath, inhaling the fragrance of the flowers Jennifer had brought him. Veronica picked up her knitting, and Dorothy resumed her crochet work. The clock on the end table ticked. Downstairs, Miss Elsie led Jennifer to the front door.

"Thank you for letting me see Captain Stone," Jennifer said graciously.

"Come back anytime, my dear. Just ask for me, if you have any trouble. Your father and I are old friends, you know."

I wonder what she meant by that, Jennifer wondered as she walked down the street back to the center of town. *Surely Daddy wouldn't patronize Miss Elsie's place, or would he?*

Jennifer knew it was difficult to understand men. She thought of John Stone lying up there with prostitutes offering him their bodies twenty-four hours a day. It'd been her impression that he hadn't been wearing any pajamas.

Jennifer may've been the mayor's daughter, and she'd own most of Petie someday, but somehow she felt inferior to the prostitutes at Miss Elsie's, because she believed they knew more about men than she.

She didn't know hardly anything about men at all. Still a virgin, her mother had died when she was little and no one had ever told her what men and women do together, although she had a general idea because she'd spent time on farms and had observed animal behavior. Prostitutes knew ways to please men that she didn't, she believed. John Stone was polite to her, but he probably thought she was just a child, compared to the women doting on him at Miss Elsie's. She imagined he'd prefer the company of experienced women to her, because men were like animals sometimes.

Maybe I'd better stay away from him for a while, she thought. *I can't make him love me, after all. All I can do is—hell—I have no idea of what to do.*

Her pretty face clouded with worry and her hands clasped

behind her back, she made her way toward the planked sidewalks of Petie.

Stone heard a stampede of footsteps on the stairs. He opened his eyes and saw that it was growing dark. He'd been asleep for several hours, he realized, and the girls evidently had left him alone because they didn't want to disturb his rest.

The footsteps came toward him across the attic. He raised himself on his elbows and saw Dr. McGrath leading a contingent of citizens that included Mayor Randlett; Thad Cooper, the lawyer and member of the town council; Clyde Akerson, manager of the Petie Savings Bank; the Reverend Vernon Scobie, pastor of the Petie Church of God; Andy Thomaston, owner of the Diamond Restaurant; and a few other men whom Stone had seen around town but didn't know personally.

"Well," said Dr. McGrath, "how's my favorite patient today? I heard you took some nourishment. Lie still and I'll check your dressing."

Stone dropped back onto the pillow, and Dr. McGrath peeled away the bandage. It hurt because the coagulated blood caused it to stick to the tender edges of the wound.

Mayor Randlett moved to the other side of the bed, holding his hat in his hands. "We want to express our appreciation for what you've done, Captain Stone. You outdrew Fritz Schuler, one of the fastest gunfighters on the frontier, and subdued the notorious Deke Casey gang that evidently was going to make another attempt on our bank. You're going to get a raise, of course, but if there's anything else you might need, don't hesitate to ask. We're all in your debt for what you've done for us."

Stone grimaced as Dr. McGrath pulled the bandage away from his skin. "I wouldn't be alive right now," he said, "if it hadn't been for Sheriff Rawlins. He saved my life, and he's the one who saved the town. He knew who Deke Casey was, and I didn't. Rawlins is a real lawman, and I was just lucky."

"Nonsense," replied Mayor Randlett. "People make their own luck. You faced down that gang all by yourself and outdrew Fritz Schuler in a fair fight. Sheriff Rawlins came along at the end and helped out, we don't deny that, but don't be so modest about your own role in the affair. Why, we've had newspapermen here from all over the frontier, and we told 'em the story. They know what the truth is. You've put this town on the map, Captain Stone. I wasn't there, and I didn't see it, but folks who were there said you were so fast they didn't even see you go for your gun. They say Fritz Schuler didn't even clear his holster when you shot him square in the chest with two close-spaced shots. Now that's marksmanship, cool under fire, steady as a rock."

Dr. McGrath peered into the wound. "Coming along real fine," he said. "You're a young man and you'll heal in no time at all."

"When do you think I'll be able to go back to work?"

Mayor Randlett held out his hand. "Don't worry about going back to work. Take your time and mend at God's own pace. Are you being well taken care of here at Miss Elsie's?"

"I get everything I need."

A few of the men guffawed. The Reverend Vernon Scobie smiled nervously. Dr. McGrath affixed a fresh bandage to Stone's shoulder. "Maybe tomorrow if you feel up to it, you might want to take a little walk. Don't push yourself, but it's good to get some exercise, keep your blood circulating, prevent bedsores, good for the liver."

Mayor Randlett looked down at Stone. "If it hadn't been for you, there's no telling what might've happened to this town."

Stone raised himself up on his elbows and look at the gathering around him. "I mean you no disrespect," he said, "but I think you're exaggerating what I did. I told you before and I'll tell you again: Sheriff Rawlins saved your bank. He's the real hero, not me. I walked straight into danger, without any idea of what I was doing, and if Sheriff Rawlins hadn't showed up, I'd be in boot hill right now. You should be thanking him, not me."

Mayor Randlett hooked his thumbs in his vest. "Gentlemen, I think we've just witnessed a fine example of what they call southern graciousness. Very well, Captain Stone, I'll go to Sheriff Rawlins first thing in the morning and thank him, but all of us here know who the real hero of the gunfight is, don't we?"

The others nodded and grunted their assent. Stone felt as if he wasn't getting through to them, but didn't feel strong enough to continue arguing. He closed his eyes and let his head sink back into the pillow.

Dr. McGrath picked up his little black bag. "I think we'd better let Captain Stone get some rest," he said. "You all can talk with him again in a few days when he's better."

They headed toward the stairs, and Stone opened one eye, watching them go. *They don't want to hear the truth*, he thought.

Sheriff Rawlins sat at his desk, raising a glass of whiskey to his lips, and Abner Pritchard looked at him disapprovingly. "Don't you think you've had enough for one day, Sheriff?"

Sheriff Rawlins was so drunk he couldn't keep both his eyes open. When one eye opened, the other would close, and when that one opened, the first one closed.

"Who the hell you think you're talkin' to?" he asked thickly.

"I'm talking to you, Sheriff. I think you've had enough."

"Who the hell cares what you think? Who told you that you know *how* to think? If I want any shit out of you, I'll knock it out of you. Till then, keep yer damn mouth shut."

"I'm just trying to tell you, Sheriff, that if there's any trouble in this town, I don't think you could handle it. Why, you can barely stand up."

"What do you mean!" Rawlins roared. "You're a goddamn liar!" To prove his point, Rawlins pushed back his chair and rose unsteadily to his feet. "There—you see? I can stand on my own two feet, so don't you ever say I can't, you little son of a bitch!"

Rawlins felt dizzy. He reached for the back of his chair to steady himself, then dropped back into it again.

"Why don't you get the hell out of here," he said to Pritchard. "Take the rest of the day off. You ain't worth a fiddler's fuck anyway."

Pritchard took off his visor and put it in his top drawer. He piled the papers neatly on his desk and got to his feet. "Are you sure there's nothing I can do for you, Sheriff?"

"I just told you what you can do for me. You can get the hell out of here and leave me alone."

Pritchard walked out of the office, and Rawlins filled up his glass again. His hand shook and the whiskey dribbled down his chin onto the desk.

He knew what was going on at Miss Elsie's. A steady stream of visitors was going up to see John Stone. Everybody was talking about how John Stone outdrew Fritz Schuler, one of the fastest gunfighters around, supposedly. Everybody was so worried about John Stone's health. *John Stone wouldn't have any health at all if it wasn't for me.*

Rawlins was furious with the citizens of Petie. As far as he was concerned, he was the one who'd subdued Deke Casey and his gang, but John Stone was getting all the credit.

Rawlins didn't want to be a hero. He just wanted the simple recognition for what he'd done, but he couldn't get it. Somehow everybody was dazzled by John Stone. They were always making such a big goddamn fuss over him.

Rawlins guzzled the glass of whiskey and poured another. He knew why everybody liked John Stone. Stone was young and good-looking, whereas Rawlins was old and said what was on his mind, and sometimes it didn't come out right. He hated the self-righteous hypocrisy of the town's leading citizens, and never tried to disguise his feelings, whereas Stone played up to those people like the two-faced bastard that he was.

I should've let them kill him, Rawlins thought, hoisting his glass of whiskey again. *Then everybody would've seen what a fraud he was.*

Toby Muldoon walked across the attic of Miss Elsie's place, a goofy smile on his face. "Hello there, Cap'n," he said. "How're you doin'?"

Stone lay in bed, his head and upper body propped up on three plush pillows. He was alone; it was another busy night at Miss Elsie's and all the girls were working downstairs.

"I'm feeling much better, Muldoon. Have a seat."

The old alcoholic sat on a chair beside the bed, his dirty knees showing through holes in his pants.

"Glad you came to see me," Stone said. "Wanted to thank you for helping me out last night. If it hadn't been for you, that galoot might've shot me."

"I was watchin' them fellers," Muldoon said in his cracked voice. "I knowed they was up to no good, so's I follered 'em. When I saw 'em set you up, I says to meself: *Toby, you got to do somethin'*, so's I hit the son of a bitch over the head with me old guitar. Now there's one thing about that guitar that I want to tell you about. It might not've looked so hot, but it had a fine sound. You ever hear that old guitar of mine?"

"I always thought it sounded real good, Muldoon."

"I knew you'd think that, because you're an edjicated man and you appreciate a good tune. Well, I took me poor ole broked guitar to the pawnshop today to see if it could be fixed, and Jay Kearney, he's the feller what runs the pawnshop, he says me old guitar cain't be fixed. So don't 'spect no more old cowboy tunes from me."

"That's no problem, Toby. We'll just get you a new one."

Toby held up his hand. "That's all right, Cap'n. You don't owe me nothin'. I'll git along without a guitar. What the hell—it's only a box with some strings attached."

"Hand me my pants."

Muldoon took Stone's pants down from a peg and handed them to Stone, who pulled a double eagle out of a pocket and flipped it to Muldoon. "Take that and buy yourself a new guitar. You saved my life and it's the least I can do."

Muldoon caught the gold coin in midair. "Naw, I couldn't take it."

"If it's not enough, tell Kearney I'll make up the difference myself."

"Could use a drink," Muldoon said, gazing longingly at the bottle on the table.

"Help yourself."

Muldoon reached for the bottle, raised it to his lips, and threw back his head, guzzling noisily, his eyes closed in ecstasy. Then he handed the bottle to Stone.

"Real good stuff you got there, Cap'n."

Stone took a swallow and returned the bottle to the table. He was trying to maintain a mild state of euphoric inebriation so his shoulder wouldn't hurt so much.

"Must be nice," Muldoon said, "livin' here with all them purty gals. Wish I could live here too, with all them purty gals."

Stone reached into his pocket and handed Muldoon more coins. "I don't suppose you can live here, but there's no reason why you can't pass some time."

"Aw, I couldn't do that, Cap'n, an old feller like me."

Muldoon stared at the coins in his hand for a few seconds, blinking his eyes. "Well, maybe I could. Thanks fer everythin', Cap'n, and I'll see you when I see you."

Muldoon adjusted his battered hat on his head and shuffled toward the stairs, reminding Stone of a spavined old warhorse who'd seen better days.

In the morning Mayor Randlett led a group of the town's leading citizens across the street toward Sheriff Rawlins's office.

"Captain Stone is right," Mayor Randlett said to them. "Sheriff Rawlins deserves our thanks for his part in the shootout with Deke Casey's gang. We've got to be fair, after all. Sheriff Rawlins is a difficult man at times, but his achievements as a law officer are first rate and quite considerable."

The other council members nodded and muttered. They were dressed in their best clothes, and waved to other citizens as they approached the door to Sheriff Rawlins's office.

"Let me do the talking," Mayor Randlett told them. "Then each and every one of us'll shake his hand, as we agreed at the meeting, and offer personal congratulations, understand?"

The council members agreed silently. None of them liked Rawlins, but John Stone's defense of the old drunken sheriff had embarrassed and prodded them into making this visit.

Mayor Randlett paused in front of the door to the office. He straightened his suit jacket, took off his hat, and opened the door.

The office appeared empty. Mayor Randlett poked his head in and looked around. "He isn't here," he said. "Maybe he's home." Then Mayor Randlett noticed a hand on the floor behind Sheriff Rawlins's desk. "Uh-oh."

He advanced into the office, and the council members followed him, holding their hats. The strong, sickly sweet odor of whiskey rose to their nostrils. They moved behind Sheriff Rawlins's desk and looked down.

Sheriff Rawlins lay on the floor, out cold, an empty bottle of whiskey beside him. A wheezing sound escaped from his nostrils every time he breathed. The council members looked at Mayor Randlett, who shook his head in dismay.

"It's a sorry sight," he said.

The mayor and members of the town council turned around and filed out of the office, leaving Sheriff Rawlins snoring on the floor behind his desk, drooling out the corner of his mouth.

8

CENTERVILLE WAS A small scattering of shacks in the middle of the prairie about a hundred miles north of Petie. All activity centered around the rickety old general store, which also was the saloon, but there wasn't much activity as a rule. A stagecoach might stop once in a while for supplies, or a wagon train might pass through, or a few cowboys could come in to buy some tobacco or a shirt, but most of the time Ben McDowell just sat around and stared out the window, as flies buzzed around his head.

Ben McDowell was seventy-one years old, with long white hair and a white mustache stained with nicotine. He placed cans of beans on a shelf, while an Indian in buckskin sat at the bar and drank a glass of whiskey. The Indian had been his only customer all day. He'd come to the store early in the morning, and now, shortly after noon, still was drinking steadily, occasionally mumbling something in his language.

McDowell heard hoofbeats on the street outside. He limped arthritically to the window and saw about thirty riders approaching the general store. They were a hard-looking bunch, dirty and unshaven, evidently cowboys moving a herd through the area and taking some time out for a drink. *Looks like I'm gonna have a busy afternoon*, McDowell thought as he moved behind the counter to greet the newcomers.

He heard them dismount outside, caught the sound of their voices as they talked among themselves. McDowell bent over and pulled bottles out of the crate, placing them on the bar.

The door was flung open, and the cowboys entered the general store, only now, at close range, they somehow didn't look like cowboys. Cowboys were basically working men, but this bunch seemed mean and wild, and they looked around suspiciously. All were armed, and some carried knives in sheaths affixed to their belts. The one in front, who evidently was their leader, was tall and slim, with slitted eyes and a thick-lipped wide mouth.

"Howdy," said McDowell with a smile. "What can I do for you gents."

"Need some supplies," the man with slitted eyes said.

"Just tell me what you want, and I'll be happy to git it for you."

"We'll git it ourselves."

The men moved toward the shelves, clearing off cans and stuffing them into gunny sacks. McDowell felt a chill come over him as he watched his store being plundered right before his eyes. One man scooped handfuls of coffee beans out of a barrel and dropped them into an empty flour sack.

The man with slitted eyes leaned his belly against the counter and looked McDowell in the eyes. "Got any money?"

"A little."

"Where's it at."

"In the strongbox."

"You'd better let me have it."

McDowell reached under the counter and came up with the steel box, which he placed on the counter. The man with slitted eyes opened it and looked at the coins.

"This all you got?"

"Yes, sir."

"You're not hidin' any back in them other rooms, are you?"

"No, sir."

The man with slitted eyes turned to one of his men. "Go back and see if you can find anythin'."

The man, who had a wide scar on his cheek, moved toward

the back rooms. Their leader counted the money and grinned.
"Ain't much."

"Don't get many customers here."

"I can see why."

The men guffawed, and McDowell tried to smile. This
wasn't the first time he'd been held up. The only thing to do
was cooperate, otherwise they'd shoot you dead. The nearest
sheriff was three days away in Metcalf.

A few feet away the Indian sipped his whiskey as if nothing
was happening. The leader of the gang noticed a newspaper
lying on a chair. He walked over and picked it up. The head-
line said:

DEKE CASEY GANG
SHOT IN PETIE

His eyes opened wide for a moment, then narrowed again
to their customary slits as he read the story. The more he read,
the crueler his features became. Then he tossed the newspaper
to one of his men. "Hey, Clint—take a look at this."

Clint, who had a squashed-down face, looked at the head-
line. "Shit—they got Casey!"

The man with slitted eyes turned to McDowell. "How far
would you say Petie is from here?"

"About a week of ridin'."

The man with the scar returned from the back rooms.
"Couldn't find no money."

The man with the slitted eyes held the newspaper in his left
hand and looked at McDowell. "Pay you back next time we
pass by this way."

McDowell nodded, trying to prevent his lips from trembling,
and a few of the outlaws laughed. The man with slitted eyes
pulled out his pistol, took quick aim at the back of the Indian,
and pulled the trigger. The cartridge exploded out of the barrel,
filling the store with gunsmoke, and the Indian got to his feet, a
red hole in the back of his buckskin jacket. Raising his hands in
the air, the Indian groaned and fell forward, landing on the floor,
writhing. The man with slitted eyes took aim at his head and
pulled the trigger, then dropped his pistol into its holster.

"Never did like injuns," he said to McDowell.

The man with slitted eyes turned and walked toward the door, and his men followed him, carrying their bags of supplies. McDowell stood behind the counter, still trembling with fear and rage. When he couldn't hear the hoofbeats of their horses anymore, he reached for one of the bottles on the counter and poured himself a drink.

"Wonder who that was," he muttered.

Jennifer Randlett stood before her father in his office and straightened his bow tie.

"I hate to do this," he said, a frown on his face.

"You've got to go through with it, Daddy," she told him. "He'll try to bully you, but you just hold your ground. You've got the entire council behind you and you simply must do what's right for this town."

"I know," he said with a sigh, "but he's been the sheriff here for so long."

Jennifer took a step back and surveyed her father's appearance. "The old days are gone, Daddy. These are the new days, and he's not doing much for us anymore. For God's sake, he's been stinking drunk for the past ten days, unable to do his job most of the time, and Captain Stone is still laid up in bed. You've got to make Sheriff Rawlins understand that he should be more responsible. It's time you and the others stood up to him." Jennifer handed her father his derby. "Now go over there and tell Sheriff Rawlins who's running this town."

Mayor Randlett took the hat and put it on his head. He kissed his daughter's forehead and left his office, crossing the street, heading toward the building where the town council met.

He wasn't anxious to confront Sheriff Rawlins, but knew it had to be done. Sheriff Rawlins had been unfit for duty ever since the shootout with the Deke Casey gang, and the town was virtually unprotected. Cowboys had been getting increasingly rambunctious, fighting in saloons, firing their pistols in the air. No one had been killed yet, but it was only a matter of time before something serious happened. The town council had agreed to take a firm hand with Sheriff Rawlins, and Mayor Randlett had to deliver the message.

Citizens said hello to him solemnly, and he tipped his hat. The whole town was tense. Everybody felt afraid. The celebration over the shootout with the Deke Casey gang had turned into a massive letdown as everyone came to realize that they were without an effective lawman.

Mayor Randlett came to a sign that said:

TOWN HALL
(upstairs)

He climbed the stairway attached to the outside of the building that also housed the Petie Savings Bank, and it was another of his real-estate holdings. He opened the door at the top and entered the town hall, a small room with a large American flag nailed to the wall. The other members of the town council sat around a long table.

"Glad to see you, Mayor," said Phineas Mathers, owner of the Double M Ranch.

Mayor Randlett nodded to him and took out his pocket watch. Sheriff Rawlins was scheduled to show up in five minutes. The atmosphere in the hall was strained. No one was looking forward to the confrontation with Sheriff Rawlins.

"Hope he'll be sober for a change," said Clyde Akerson, manager of the Petie Savings Bank.

"I wouldn't bet on that," replied the Reverend Vernon Scobie, a sour expression on his face.

"Here he comes," said Martin Caldwell, proprietor of Caldwell's General Store, who was standing next to the window and looking down at the street.

Mayor Randlett took his seat at the middle of the table. He leaned back in the chair and sipped a glass of water. Caldwell returned to his chair also. They heard the sound of footsteps on the stairs attached to the building. The footsteps were heavy and made the building shake slightly. The members of the town council shifted uneasily in their chairs. All were scared to death of Sheriff Rawlins.

The door opened and Sheriff Rawlins stood in front of them, his face flushed, his clothing rumpled, and his tin badge pinned to his lapel. An expression of contempt and malevolence was on his face as he advanced toward the table where the town council sat. The air was so thick it could be cut with an axe.

Mayor Randlett tried to smile. "Hello, Sheriff Rawlins—

glad you could come." He gestured toward the chairs scattered in front of the table for the comfort of those who brought business or testified before the town council.

Sheriff Rawlins glowered at him. "I'll stand."

Now that Sheriff Rawlins was close to the table, the town councilmen could smell whiskey and see the glassy haze in his eyes. He was teetering slightly, and his shirt was partially untucked.

"What the hell do you want with me!" Sheriff Rawlins roared.

Mayor Randlett looked up at him and tried to gather together his courage. "Sheriff Rawlins," he said, "we've asked you here because we're concerned about the deteriorating quality of law and order in Petie. We feel that you haven't been attending to your duties properly lately, and we'd like to voice our concern about that to you, if you don't mind."

Sheriff Rawlins closed his eyes for three long seconds, then opened them up again. "What the hell are you talkin' about, Randlett! You don't like the way I'm doin' my job?"

Mayor Randlett thought of Jennifer, and about how annoyed she'd be if he didn't stand up to Rawlins. Mayor Randlett cleared his throat and said as clearly and steadily as he could: "That's right—we don't like the way you've been performing your duties. You've been drunk for most of the past ten days, leaving the townspeople at the mercy of bullies and rowdies who fight with each other and shoot their guns randomly at whatever targets they see. It's got to stop, Sheriff Rawlins. We know you're a competent lawman, and we know you can establish control if you want to. That's why we're having this little talk with you. We want you to cut down on your drinking and start performing the duties we're paying you to perform, otherwise we'll have to look elsewhere for our protection. We don't want you to think we're threatening you, but we . . . "

"Threatening me!" Rawlins shouted. "You goddamn well better not threaten me!" He took two steps closer to the table, and Mayor Randlett wanted to get up and run. "Now you listen to me, you bunch of *old ladies!* That's right—I said *ladies!* That's all you are to me! Not one of you's got any balls! Let me tell you something, *ladies!* I made all of you what you are today—*with this!*" Sheriff Rawlins yanked out his pistol and waved it in the air. "That's right!" Rawlins hollered drunkenly. "If it wasn't for me and my gun, there wouldn't be any goddamn town here! You owe everything you own to me, and what do I get out of it after twenty years of puttin' my neck on the block for you every day? Two hundred dollars a month, which is the same as what you pay my deputy after he was in town *two fuckin' hours!*" He pointed his finger at Mayor Randlett. "If you want to fire me, then goddamn it—fire me! But don't you ever tell me what to do again! I do what I goddamn please around here! And if you ever want to talk to me again, see me in my office! From now on you come to me—I don't come to you!"

Andy Thomaston, owner of the Diamond Restaurant, was raising a glass of water to his lips. Sheriff Rawlins took quick aim with his pistol and pulled the trigger. The glass exploded in Thomaston's hand, and he shrieked in terror.

Sheriff Rawlins holstered his pistol, swung around, and staggered out the door, leaving the town council of Petie in stunned silence.

The gang sat around their campfires, eating beans and bacon, drinking coffee and smoking cigarettes, passing the newspaper around. Their horses were picketed nearby, grazing on prairie grass. They were about twenty miles from Centerville in open country, and they had lookouts posted just in case.

The man with the slitted eyes was Brad Culhane, and he'd known Deke Casey well. Culhane had ridden with Bloody Bill Anderson during the war, and knew all the members of Deke Casey's gang.

His gang was similar to Deke Casey's, only it operated on a larger scale. Their principle means of support was cattle rustling across the length and breadth of the frontier. There were enough of them to take over entire herds and drive them to market, and buyers usually weren't fussy about where their stock came from, as long as it was in good condition and the price was right.

Culhane and his men had just finished rustling a herd in Montana, and now were drifting south, looking for new opportunities, when they'd come upon that newspaper in the general store in Centerville.

Everybody in Culhane's bunch was incensed by the story. It said that the sheriff and deputy of a town called Petie had wiped out the entire Deke Casey gang with the assistance of some local citizens. The reporter had written eloquently of the skill and fighting courage of the sheriff and deputy, and the blundering ineptness of Deke Casey and his men, who were represented as a group of vicious clowns.

Jubal Davidge, who wore a wide scar on his cheek, threw the newspaper to the ground at Culhane's feet. "Those sons of bitches!" he said, and spat into the fire. "I say we should go down there and burn their goddamn town to the ground!"

Several of the men growled their agreement, chewing their food angrily, all in rotten moods.

Clint Fulton, who had a squashed-down face, was rolling a cigarette. "We can't let 'em get away with it," he said. "It ain't right what them people done to Deke and the boys."

"We all fought together in the war," said Sand Kelley, another member of the gang. "They was our friends, and them people kilt them. I think we should go down there to Petie and show them people they can't kill our friends and git away with it!"

The other men grumbled angrily. The destruction of Deke Casey and his gang was a personal insult to them, and they wanted revenge.

Culhane rose to his feet and looked at them. "You sure that's what you want to do!"

"You're damn right," said Davidge, and the rest of the gang nodded their approval, standing and gathering around Culhane.

Culhane looked at them, his thick lips set in a grim line. They were all killers, thieves, and cutthroats, but they'd fought together in the war and were bound together by pride, common feelings, and deeds written in blood.

"I knew Deke pretty good," Culhane told them. "We was like brothers almost, and I know what he'd do if it happened to us. He'd do what we're gonna do. He'd wipe that town off the face of the map. Is that the way you see it, boys?"

"Yeah!" they replied, squaring their shoulders and balling up their fists.

"Then let's go to Petie!" Culhane replied. "And God help the people who live there, because there ain't gonna be nothin' left of 'em when we git finished! They'll be sorry they ever heard of Deke Casey!"

"Hell," said Davidge, "when we git finished with 'em, they'll be sorry they was ever born!"

John Stone walked down the hill toward the center of Petie, wearing both his Colts in his crisscrossed gunbelts, and his knife in his boot, feeling nearly the way he did before he'd been shot.

He'd been up and around Miss Elsie's place for five days, shooting cans in the backyard, eating like a horse, getting his strength back. He'd done a little carpentry work for Miss Elsie, and all the girls had made a big fuss over him, giving him anything he wanted, and offering him special favors in subtle and not so subtle ways, but he always managed to resist somehow.

It was a cloudy day and looked as though it might rain. As he approached the Olympia Hotel, he had a moment of light-headedness, but it passed and he continued on his way to the sheriff's office.

The townspeople spotted his tall muscular form moving toward them, and they stopped to stare. Children ran toward him and jumped up and down gleefully. Their elders followed, shyly at first, then advancing closer. A man shook his hand and patted him on the back.

A crowd gathered around Stone, stopping him on the sidewalk. Everyone was talking at once, excited to be in his presence. Dogs barked and ran back and forth in the street. Somebody let out a cheer. They'd read about his exploits in newspapers published in big cities, and he was their hero.

Stone was embarrassed and wished he could hide someplace, but there was nowhere to go. He had to stand and take it, and didn't want to hurt anybody's feelings. The people were all talking at once, telling him what a great man he was and how much they appreciated what he'd done for them.

Stone responded to their remarks politely, in his soft-spoken way. He was ill at ease and wished they'd go away. It was as though they wanted to devour him with their eyes, and absorb some of him into themselves just by being in his presence.

Toby Muldoon stumbled around the edge of the crowd,

plunking his new guitar, but it sounded out of tune just like his old one.

Across the street in the sheriff's office, Sheriff Rawlins heard the commotion. He got to his feet and walked unsteadily to the window, to see what was going on. He looked outside, saw the crowd, and spotted John Stone standing in the middle of it, towering over the people, his wide-brimmed cavalry hat on his head.

Jealousy and resentment filled Sheriff Rawlins's heart. With a curse he turned around and stomped back to his desk, sitting down and raising the whiskey bottle to his lips. The office smelled like a saloon. Rawlins emptied the bottle of whiskey and tossed it in his wastebasket, which was full of other empty bottles.

He turned down the corners of his mouth as he listened to the sounds of the townspeople across the street, making a fuss over John Stone. "Why that goddamn son of a bitch," he said aloud. "If it hadn't been for me, he'd be dead."

The resentment and pain bubbled in his heart. He was hurt by the way the townspeople had turned from him to John Stone. They'd admired him so much in the old days, bought him drinks and meals, and the kids tagged along after him when he walked down the street. Now they treated him like a piece of old junk.

He opened his desk drawer, to get another bottle of whiskey, but the drawer was empty. He'd have to go out and buy some more, but didn't want to use the front door, where the people could see him. He put on his hat and headed for the rear exit, passing the mirror, catching a glimpse of himself and trying not to be dismayed by what he saw. His eyes had become sunken and his clothes hung loosely on his gaunt body. He'd lost nearly twenty pounds.

He stumbled down the back alley, passing sheds and outhouses. A spotted dog tied to a tree barked at him. He came to the rear of the Paradise Saloon and went inside. The customers looked at him apprehensively, and those at the bar moved away as he approached.

"Whiskey," he said in a hoarse voice.

Doreen Eckles was on duty, and she set him up with a glass and a bottle. He picked up the glass and flung it across the room. It hit the far wall and shattered, the men nearby holding up their arms to shield themselves from the falling shards of glass.

He picked up the bottle and carried it to the nearest table, where four men were playing draw poker.

"Get the hell out of my way!" he roared.

The card players got up from the table and retreated. Sheriff Rawlins dropped onto one of the chairs, pulled the cork out of the bottle, upended it, and drank deeply.

The room spun around him. He burped, cursed, and drank some more. A terrible sinking sensation was in his stomach and he felt as if he were falling through the floor and into a tunnel that led to the center of the earth. "I hate you goddamn sons of bitches," he uttered darkly. "I made you what you are."

He kicked the nearest empty chair, and it went flying across the room. An ashtray full of cigar and cigarette butts sat in the middle of his table, and he picked up the ashtray, hurling it into the air. The ashes and butts fell on people nearby, and they scattered out of the way.

"I gave my life to this town," he grumbled. "I stood up for you damn shitbirds when you was too scared to stand up for yourselves. Every day I risked my neck for you, and what did you ever do for me? Not a goddamn fuckin' thing, that's what."

He raised the bottle of whiskey to his lips and thought of John Stone. "That dumb son of a bitch. If it hadn't been for me he'd be pushing up daisies right now. Everybody thinks he's so damn great. Well, he ain't nothin'—you hear? He ain't nothin'!"

Rawlins looked around him and was surprised to see that the saloon had become empty, except for Doreen Eckles behind the bar. He blinked his eyes, took off his hat, and scratched his head, feeling uneasy and sick. He hadn't even seen them go. *Must've blacked out again.*

"I think I'm goin' home," he said. "Don't feel so good."

He put on his hat, stood, walked three steps, and bumped into a table, knocking it over. He fell to his hands and knees, shouted incoherently, and climbed to his feet again. He made his way to the doors and found himself out on the sidewalk.

He put his hands in his pockets and looked down the street, trying to focus, and saw the crowd still gathered around John

Stone. A few riders passed by in the middle of the street. Rawlins was seized with the mad urge to walk down there and shoot John Stone, but a more rational part of his mind took over and told him that was a bad idea.

He stood on the sidewalk, wiping his mouth with the back of his hand, reeling. There was something he'd wanted to do, but forgot what it was. He decided to go back to his office and lie down, then remembered what he'd wanted to do. He had to go to the liquor store and get another bottle.

He crossed the street, his hat crooked on his head, and he had the feeling that his pants were falling down. He pulled them up, lost his footing in the mud and muck in the middle of the street, and fell down.

Somehow he couldn't get up. He tried, but his hands wouldn't work and neither would his knees. He was aware that he was rolling around in the mud, growling like a dog. Somebody laughed nearby.

"Lookit Sheriff Rawlins!" a woman said.

Somehow he got to his feet, but he was covered with mud from head to foot. "Gotta go home," he said.

He blinked his eyes. A group of people had gathered around, staring at him with dismay.

"Get the hell away from me. I got no use for any of yez."

Suddenly the world went black again, and he felt himself falling. Wind whistled past his ears and he heard the sound of bells tinkling in the distance. He dropped into that deep dark tunnel again, and everything became still.

Sometime later, Rawlins opened his eyes and realized that he was lying on his bed. Rosie sat on the chair next to him.

"Are you all right?" she asked.

"How'd I get home?" he asked weakly.

"You walked here, and I helped you."

"Don't remember a thing," he said, rubbing his forehead with the palm of his hand.

"You've got to stop drinkin', Buck. It's killin' you."

"Mind yer goddamn business, woman."

"The people in this town aren't going to put up with yer shenanigans much longer. If you don't sober up, they're gonna fire you."

"Like hell they will," Rawlins said. "Them lily-livered bastards wouldn't dare."

"You're pushin' 'em awful hard."

"And I'll push 'em harder. I made this town, don't you forget that. If they they try to fire me, there'll be hell to pay."

"You gentlemen wanted to see me?" John Stone asked.

He was standing in front of the town council in their office above the Petie Savings Bank, and the members were lined up behind their long table, sitting in their armchairs, drinking whiskey and smoking cigars.

Mayor Randlett sat in the chair with the tallest back, in the middle of the others. His round belly was covered by a neatly buttoned vest, with a gold watch chain hanging across it.

"We've decided to bite the bullet," Mayor Randlett said to Stone. "We're going to fire Sheriff Rawlins, and we wondered if you'd take over his job while we're looking for somebody to replace him."

"I'd like to move on," Stone said. "My month'll be up pretty soon."

"We're in a difficult position, John. Sheriff Rawlins isn't performing his duties at all anymore, as you know, and if you leave, we won't have any law here at all."

"You could form a committee and be your own lawmen, until you find somebody."

Mayor Randlett smiled. "We're not gunfighters. We're businessmen, ranchers, lawyers, merchants. We need a professional to maintain law and order in Petie. I know you said you'd only stay for a month, but we were wondering if you'd give us another month, in view of the circumstances. We'd double your salary and pick up any expenses you might incur. That'd give us the time we need to search out a new sheriff."

John Stone thought of all the friends he'd made in Petie, the girls at Miss Elsie's place, and old Toby Muldoon. He couldn't leave them vulnerable to thieves, gunmen, and bullies. The double salary would provide him with a good solid stake for his continuing search for Marie, and the extra time would permit him to recover fully from his wound before facing the hardships of the trail.

"All right," he said, "but I want you to understand that this is my last extension, and I'm leaving when my time is up whether you've got another lawman or not."

The council members looked at one another and smiled. Mayor Randlett got to his feet. "Thank you, John," he said. "We appreciate your help, and we won't forget it." He turned to the other members of the town council. "Gentlemen, now all we have to do is fire Sheriff Rawlins." He turned and faced Stone again. "Do you think you could accompany us to Sheriff Rawlins's home, John?"

"I'm afraid you'll have to do that on your own, Mayor. I don't want any part of firing Sheriff Rawlins."

There was a knock on the door, and Rosie opened her eyes. It was late afternoon and she was lying in bed with her clothes on, next to Rawlins who'd been passed out since morning.

She rolled out of bed, fussed with her hair in front of a mirror for a few seconds, and opened the front door. Standing before her were Mayor Randlett and several members of the town council. In a flash she knew what they wanted. She'd been expecting this all week.

"We'd like to speak with him, Rosie," Mayor Randlett said gently.

"He's asleep right now."

"It's important."

She sighed, because she knew the inevitable couldn't be postponed. "Come on in," she said. "I'll git him up."

They entered the room, which was furnished with a stove and a square table with two chairs. The floor and walls were of rough unpainted wood. Stale cooking odors were in the air, along with cigarette smoke and the smell of whiskey.

Rosie entered the bedroom and closed the door. She bent over Rawlins and shook his shoulder. "Get up," she said firmly. "Come on, Buck—open yer eyes."

He looked up at her. "What the hell do you want?"

"They're here. Mayor Randlett and the town council."

Sheriff Rawlins blinked. He was half drunk and half hungover, his mouth like cotton and his head throbbing with pain. He'd been expecting this, but had been too sick and drunk to do anything about it. He reached for his bottle. "Tell 'em I'll be right there."

He took a few swallows, then got out of bed and pulled on his pants. He'd hoped it wouldn't come to this, that a miracle would happen and somehow everything'd be all right, but knew he'd been going too far lately and it couldn't continue forever. He felt strangely contrite as he sucked on the bottle again. Then he put on his frock coat with the badge pinned on the lapel. Standing erectly, he opened the door and stepped into the kitchen.

They stood on the other side of the table, the wealthiest and most influential men in Petie, and Sheriff Rawlins felt embarrassed in his dingy little home with the rickety furniture and dreary odors. It was like a bad dream.

"You wanted to see me, gentlemen?" he said, his voice cracking.

Mayor Randlett held his hat in his hands and fidgeted with the brim. "I'm sorry, Sheriff Rawlins, but we've taken a vote and decided that we'll have to ask for your badge."

Sheriff Rawlins felt as if his knees would give out. Glancing toward Rosie, he saw tears rolling down her cheeks. He wanted to get mad, but somehow the anger wouldn't come.

Mayor Randlett continued to speak. "I'm sorry it's come to this, Sheriff Rawlins. You've done wonderful things for this town, but it's no good anymore." He held out his hand. "Could you give me your badge?"

Sheriff Rawlins felt like a mechanical toy as he reached toward his lapel and unpinned his badge, dropping it into Mayor Randlett's hand.

"If you can get yourself sober and straighten yourself out, we'll be glad to have you back," Mayor Randlett said. "If you need any help with anything, just call on any one of us here, and we'll be glad to give you a hand." Mayor Randlett reached into the inner pocket of his suit jacket and took out an envelope. "Here's a check for two months' pay, to tide you over. Good luck to you, Buck. I hope you understand that we had to do this—you gave us no choice."

Mayor Randlett and the other members of the town council turned around and walked out the door. They headed toward the center of town, and Mayor Randlett lit a cigar. "That wasn't hard at all," he said. "I thought he took it real well, don't you?"

• • •

Rawlins sat at the kitchen table and stared out the window at the sky. Rosie stood beside the stove and sobbed into a handkerchief. Rawlins wondered where his life had gone. He'd grown up on a farm in Georgia, roamed the frontier, cleaned up Petie, fought for Bobby Lee in the war, and then became sheriff of Petie for the second time, giving Petie a total of twenty years of his life, and the time had gone so quickly. Now suddenly he was an old man with no future and no plans. He felt numb, like a statue.

After a while he went to the bedroom and got his bottle of whiskey, bringing it back to the table.

"Buck," said Rosie, "don't drink no more. It ain't gonna do you no good."

He didn't answer her, he just uncorked the bottle and gulped some down. He felt empty and sick, like the day the word came down that Bobby Lee had surrendered to Grant at Appomattox. As on that day, he didn't know what to do with himself.

He continued to drink throughout the afternoon, and finally Rosie had to go to work.

"Don't git in no trouble, Buck," she told him, kissing his cheek. "We can work it all out together."

When he looked up again, she was gone. He finished off the bottle and took another out of the cupboard, uncorking it, raising it in the air, and kissing its lips.

The burning liquid flowed into his body, stimulating his memory. He thought of drunks he'd thrown in jail, gunmen he'd faced down, thieves he'd apprehended. So many years he'd given to the people of Petie, and now they'd fired him just because he drank a little too much. Somehow it didn't seem fair.

He had scars all over his body from fights and bullet wounds he'd received while upholding law and order in Petie. Rich men like Randlett and the members of the town council got richer, and he just got older and more beat up. They'd never cared about him—they'd just used him the way they'd use a plowhorse, but when a plowhorse got old it was turned out to pasture, whereas Rawlins was getting two months' pay and that was it.

"Them sons of bitches," he said, and felt his anger returning. "Look at how they treated me, after all I done for them."

• • •

Mayor Randlett walked into the sheriff's office and saw Stone sitting behind the desk, trying to make sense of the correspondence that was piling up.

"We did it," Mayor Randlett said. He took Rawlins's badge out of his vest pocket. "This is yours now. Put it on."

"Save it for the next man you hire."

"You're the sheriff around here now."

"I don't want Rawlins's badge."

"What're you doing there?"

"Paperwork."

"Bring it to Jennifer in the morning. She'll take care of it for you."

Mayor Randlett left the office, and Stone stared out the glass door at riders passing on the street. *Poor son of a bitch*, he thought. *Wonder how he's going to handle it*.

It got dark, and Rawlins continued drinking and brooding. "I should've thrown the badge right in their damned faces," he said. "I should've stood up to them, but instead I backed down like a coward."

He finished the bottle and lurched toward the cupboard for more, but no more whiskey was left. Cursing, he punched his fist into the wall, bloodying his knuckles. His hand hurt, but something deep inside him hurt more. He looked around and felt trapped. That horrible sinking feeling came to him again, as if he was going to pass out. "I've got to get out of here," he said.

He strapped on his gun, put on his hat, and left his house. It was pitch-black outside, clouds covered the moon and stars. In the distance he could see the lights of the downtown saloon district. He headed in that direction, muttering and cursing. The cool breeze against his face enlivened him somewhat, and the sinking feeling was gone. He was confused, angry, and starting to feel wild. "Them goddamn bastards," he said. "Them sons of whores."

He found himself in front of the Paradise Saloon, and piano music came from inside. He walked through the swinging doors and saw the usual scene that he'd known so well for twenty years.

The bartender saw him coming and placed a bottle and a glass on the bar. Rawlins threw the glass over his shoulder, and it landed in the middle of a table where five men were playing draw poker. They jumped, saw Rawlins, and decided not to make an issue of it. Everybody was afraid of him when he was drunk.

He drank from the mouth of the bottle and leaned over the bar. Taking out a stogie, he lit it up and blew smoke in the air. Then he swallowed more whiskey, trying to make the pain go away, but it wouldn't go away.

He turned around and faced the men sitting at the tables. "You bastards finally got rid of old Sheriff Rawlins!" he hollered. "Hope you feel better now!"

He carried the bottle to a table against the far wall where three men were drinking and carrying on a conversation.

"Get the hell away from me," he growled.

They got up and moved to another table. Rawlins sat down heavily and continued drinking and smoking. When his stogie was down to the stub he threw it in the cuspidor a few feet away. His face was blotched, his hat was crooked on his head, and spittle leaked out of the corner of his mouth.

He continued drinking, and the hours passed. Rawlins thought about the war, cannons firing, attacks and counterattacks, blood and guts everywhere, and battlefields where you couldn't put your foot down without stepping on a dead body. He recalled when he'd first come to Petie, and the townspeople had begged him to be their sheriff. He hadn't even wanted the job, but figured what the hell, maybe it was time he stopped drifting. The people seemed to need him so badly, the women and kids were so scared, and regular pay every month seemed like a good idea for a change.

He was vaguely aware of men moving around him, coming and going, throwing cards onto tables, laughing, having a good time. "It's as if I ain't even here," he mumbled. "Nobody gives a shit about me anymore."

Suddenly a hush fell over the Paradise Saloon. Rawlins looked up and saw John Stone walking toward the bar, the tin badge pinned to the front of his shirt.

All Rawlins's resentment became focused on Stone, who

now had his job. Everything had been okay for Rawlins before John Stone came to town.

"Well, look who's here!" Rawlins hollered. "The fastest gun alive, only he wouldn't be alive right now if it wasn't for—for . . . " Rawlins lost his train of thought and wrinkled his brow, trying to get it back again, but it wouldn't come.

Stone turned and looked at Rawlins, sitting disheveled and drunk at his table. He didn't want to ignore Rawlins, but didn't want to talk with him either.

"You're a fuckin' weasel!" Rawlins called out to Stone. "Everybody thinks you're so great, but I could whip you now, I could whip you tomorrow, I could whip you anytime I wanted, name yer weapons, rough and tumble, whatever!"

Rawlins blinked when he realized that Stone was walking toward him. He rose to his feet and pulled back the right side of his frock coat, so he could draw his pistol. He thought Stone was going to challenge him to a gunfight!

Stone stopped a few feet from Rawlins's table. "You saved my life," he said. "I haven't had a chance to thank you yet, so I'm thanking you now."

"Shove yer thanks up yer ass. I wouldn't trust you as far as I could throw you. Everybody around here thinks you're so goddamned fast. Well show 'em how fast you are. Go for yer gun, if you got the guts."

"I'm not going to draw on you, Sheriff."

"Well, I'm gonna draw on you."

In a sudden movement, Rawlins yanked out his pistol and pointed it at Stone's chest. Behind Stone, men rose from their chairs and got out of the way.

"You stole my job," Rawlins said drunkenly.

Stone looked at the barrel of Rawlins's gun. "I didn't steal your job. I'm only the deputy, and I'm leaving this town as soon as I can. You didn't lose your job because of me. You lost your job because you're a drunk."

Rawlins thought Stone must be crazy to talk to him that way when he was aiming a loaded gun at his chest. Rawlins was unnerved by what John Stone said. He held his aim steady on Stone's chest and felt Stone's eyes burning into his brain.

"Aw, to hell with you," Rawlins said, lowering his pistol. "You ain't worth a bullet."

Rawlins collapsed into his chair. A dizzy spell came over him, and when he opened his eyes again, Stone was gone. Men were playing cards and drinking all around him, and he realized he'd blacked out again. He wondered if he'd really seen Stone, or if he'd dreamed him. Sometimes it was hard for him to know what was real and what wasn't.

He continued to drink, and the night rolled on. When his bottle was empty he careened toward the bar and got another, returning to the table and pulling out the cork. He gulped down more and felt sleepy. Closing his eyes, he leaned back in his chair, holding the bottle in his right hand.

"Come on home, Buck."

Rawlins opened his eyes. His face lay in a puddle of whiskey and drool on the table. He straightened up and wiped his cheek with his sleeve, then turned and saw Rosie beside him, tugging his sleeve.

"It's time to go to bed, Buck. Let's go."

"Get yer goddamn hands off'n me, woman!"

Rawlins drew himself away from her and reached for the bottle.

She pulled it off the table before he could touch it. "You had enough," she told him. "You keep drinkin' like this, you'll kill yerself. Let's go home. I'll make you some coffee."

"Gimme that bottle!"

With a vicious snarl he lunged forward and pulled the bottle out of her hand.

"Goddamn woman, always tryin' to tell a man what to do."

"Please, Buck—don't drink no more tonight." Tears welled up in her eyes. "I'm afraid somethin' bad's gonna happen."

"Get the hell away from me! I'm tired of lookin at yer goddamn ugly face!"

He reached over and pushed her, and her chair tipped over. She fell to the floor.

He saw her out of the corner of his eye, picking herself up off the floor, and he knew he'd just done something terrible, but he was hurting deep inside and somehow it made him feel better to know that she was hurting too.

She got to her feet and stood a few feet in front of him, her lips trembling. "I'm gonna tell you somethin', Buck, and I'm just gonna tell it to you once. This's been goin' on for long enough now, and I can't live with it anymore. If you don't come home with me now, you'd better not never come home again, because I ain't lettin' you in."

"Get the hell away from me," he said. "Who needs you anyways?"

His words were slurred and the corners of his mouth were turned down in derision. She wiped her eyes with her hands and turned away, heading for the door. It was quiet in the saloon, and everyone had heard each word. Rawlins watched her go and realized he'd humiliated her. He wished he hadn't done it, and thought maybe he should run after her, but a man should never run after a woman, and when he looked again, she was gone.

He reached for the bottle and drank until he wasn't thinking about Rosie anymore. He stared into space and remembered his childhood in Georgia. His father had been a sharecropper, and they'd had a hard life. They hadn't owned any slaves, they worked the land themselves, from early in the morning till late at night. He'd had five brothers and sisters, and there was always something to do. They raised cotton, and most of it went to the landlord. Rawlins and the other members of his family barely had enough to eat, they wore rags and lived in a shack.

John Stone reminded him of the sons of his landlord. While Rawlins worked in the fields every day, the landlord's sons didn't do anything except hunt, fish, and have fun. Rawlins had hated his landlord's sons, and maybe that was one of the reasons he hated Stone.

It was two o'clock in the morning, and most of the customers in the saloon had gone home. Only a few serious drinkers remained, seated here and there at tables, and one held a noisy argument with the bartender about the quality of whiskey.

The hours passed, and Rawlins continued to sip whiskey. A few times he fell asleep for short stretches, and when he awoke the first thing he did was reach for the bottle again. He sank more deeply into wrath and indignation against the townspeople and John Stone, as if they were conspiring against him, trying to destroy him. "I hate 'em all," he muttered. "They can all go to hell, for all I care."

He especially despised John Stone, whom he considered a liar and a sneak. "He stole my job." John Stone had turned the town against him. "I should've let Deke Casey and his boys shoot him down."

Rawlins fell asleep again, his head lying on the table, and when he opened his eyes he saw the first glimmer of the new day. A man in a dirty white apron swept out the saloon and emptied the cuspidors. Rawlins finished his bottle of whiskey, then stumbled toward the bar and got a cup of coffee. He carried the cup to his table, spilling nearly half the coffee in the saucer, and sat facing the door. He slurped the coffee out of the saucer, then sipped from the cup. Something told him he ought to eat something, but he didn't feel hungry.

He had a stomachache, a headache, and his throat hurt. The coffee made his heart beat faster. He saw the first customers of the new day enter the saloon, and Doreen Eckles replaced the night bartender. Everything started spinning around Rawlins's head. He felt as though he was going to vomit, and closed his eyes.

When he opened his eyes again he was sprawled back in his chair, his head lolling back and his mouth open. The saloon was noisy and crowded, and he realized a considerable amount of time had passed. He straightened up in his chair and saw a fly in his empty cup of coffee.

Something fluttered in his stomach, and his ears were ringing. *I need a drink*, he said to himself. He got up and staggered to the bar.

"Whiskey," he said.

Doreen Eckles placed the bottle and glass in front of him. He reached into his pocket for the money, and his pocket was empty.

"Run out of money," he said. "Pay you later on in the day."

She pointed to the sign behind her: NO CREDIT.

He smiled unsteadily. "That don't mean me. I'm the sheriff. I been in this town for twenny years."

"I don't care how long you been here," Doreen Eckles said, "no credit."

"I got money in that bank over there. All I gotta do is go git it."

"Go ahead and git it. I'll hold yer bottle for you."

"You don't trust me," Rawlins snarled, placing his hand on the butt of his pistol.

"No credit," she replied. "It's the rules of the house."

Rawlins felt like shooting her, but he couldn't shoot a woman. He felt as if the whole world was against him. Spitting into a cuspidor, he pulled up his pants and headed for the door. The other customers in the Paradise stared at him, because they'd never seen him like this before. His clothes were rumpled, he needed a shave, and his complexion had a deathly pallor. He stepped onto the sidewalk and it was another cloudy day. Everything went black for several seconds, and when he came to he was crossing the street, heading toward the Petie Savings Bank.

He knew he was in bad shape. People looked at him with expressions of disgust or disapproval and it only made him more defiant. "Fuck yez all!" he muttered. "Yez can all kiss my ass if you don't like what I'm doin'."

He approached the front of the Petie Savings Bank, just as Thad Cooper stepped out the door. He turned toward Rawlins and wrinkled his brow as he remembered the night Rawlins had slapped his face and humiliated him in the Acme Saloon.

"Well, look who's here!" Rawlins roared. "One of the Petie's foremost liars!"

Cooper looked Rawlins over, and the former sheriff of Petie appeared to be in a state of deep stupefaction, wobbling from side to side, and his handlebar mustaches were frazzled and bent out of shape, making him seem ridiculous. Cooper ordinarily would've been afraid of Rawlins, but Rawlins looked harmless now.

"Go home and sleep it off," Cooper said to him. "You're drunk."

Rawlins's bloodshot eyes widened at the insult. "What did you say to me?"

"I said go home and sleep it off. You're drunk."

"You can't talk to me that way—you goddamned four-flusher!"

Cooper looked at Rawlins contemptuously. Rawlins appeared barely able to stand, and his clothes were dirty and wrinkled. "I and every other citizen in this town are sick of your insults and bad manners," Cooper said. "Why don't you just shut up for a change."

Cooper moved to walk past Rawlins, and Rawlins raised his
hands, pushing Cooper's chest hard, forcing Cooper to take a
few steps backward.

"You son of a bitch!" Rawlins said murderously. "Who the
hell do you think you're talkin' to!"

Cooper smoothed down the front of his shirt. A crowd was
forming, and Cooper didn't want to be humiliated publicly
again, particularly by a man who looked as though he was
ready to pass out on his feet.

Cooper thrust out his jaw and walked toward Rawlins, who
raised his hands to push Cooper as he did last time, but this
time Cooper's reflexes were faster, and he pushed first.

Rawlins went flying backward. He struggled to regain his
balance, but somehow his feet wouldn't obey his orders. He
fell off the sidewalk and landed in a pile of horse manure in
the street.

The crowd laughed, and Rawlins coughed at the smell of the
manure. He looked up and saw the faces of the townspeople
creased in mirth. A deep, slow rage came over him. These
were the people he'd protected for twenty years, and they were
treating him like a buffoon. His heart felt like it was breaking
with pain and shame.

He scrambled to his feet. "Cooper!" he shouted.

He focused on the sidewalk and saw Cooper walking away,
ignoring him, and that was yet another insult. Rawlins's brain
became icy clear. He couldn't let somebody treat him that way
and get away with it.

He jumped onto the sidewalk and ran after Cooper, who
heard him coming and turned around.

Cooper felt as though he had the upper hand now. He thought
Rawlins was drunk and stupid, no longer dangerous, a fool and
the object of everybody's scorn.

"What do you want?" Cooper asked.

Rawlins faced him on the sidewalk, ten feet away. "You
don't treat me this way," he said hoarsely.

"I'll treat you the way you deserve to be treated. You're
a loudmouth and a bully, and this town has had enough of
you."

Rawlins smiled. "You're awful brave today, Cooper. How
come you're so brave all of a sudden?"

"You're not pushing me around anymore. I've had it with you."

"You have, eh?" Rawlins took a step back and spread his legs apart, holding his right hand loose in the air. "Well, do somethin' about it."

Cooper was carrying a Smith & Wesson pistol in a holster underneath his frock coat, and knew how to use it. Under ordinary circumstances, he'd never draw on Rawlins, but now Rawlins was tottering from side to side, and had horse manure all over his pants.

"I couldn't shoot a drunk in cold blood," Cooper said.

"You're gonna have to."

Cooper looked around and saw the nearby townspeople heading for shelter in the alleys. There was a crowd on the other side of the street.

"Somebody git the sheriff!" a voice shouted.

Rawlins stared at Cooper. "I'm gonna kill you, you son of a bitch."

"Rawlins, I don't think you realize how drunk you are."

"You're a damned coward and everybody knows it!"

Cooper's face flushed with anger. "Who're you calling a coward!"

"You!"

"You need somebody to teach you a lesson, you old fool."

"Why don't you teach it to me, Cooper?"

"Don't tempt me."

"You're a weakling and an old woman, like everybody else in this goddamn town. You ain't got the guts to draw on me."

"Don't push me, Rawlins."

"I'm gonna count to three," Rawlins said. "*One*."

"Now wait a minute!"

"*Two*."

Cooper didn't see any way out of it. He realized he'd have to shoot Rawlins or be shot by him, but didn't think he could lose. The old ex-sheriff was drunk as the lord.

"*Three!*"

Cooper reached for his gun and saw to his horror that Rawlins already was drawing a bead on his chest. Rawlins's pistol fired, and Cooper felt a firestorm in his chest before he had a chance to draw his pistol. He fell back against a post, blood burbling out of his mouth, and Rawlins shot him again. The impact of the bullet sent Cooper spinning around. His hat fell off his head and he dropped to the sidewalk, twitching a few times, and then he became still.

Rawlins dropped his pistol into his holster and walked toward Cooper, kicking him over onto his back. Rawlins felt sober and steady as a rock, just like in the old days.

"Who's next?" he asked.

He looked around, and the townspeople cowered in the alleys, afraid to come out.

"So you think I'm over the hill, do you?" he asked. "Well, I ain't finished yet. You think you can laugh at me? Well, go ahead and laugh at me, and see what'll happen if you do."

Nobody laughed or said a word. Clyde Akerson came out of the bank, kneeled beside Cooper, and felt his pulse. "He's dead."

Rawlins looked at blood spreading over Cooper's ruffled white shirt. "Sure he's dead. He drawed on me."

"His gun's not even out of his holster."

"You callin' me a liar?"

Akerson didn't answer. He was looking over the hitching rail. Rawlins followed his eyes and saw a lone figure advancing down the center of the street, wearing high-topped black boots with his jeans tucked into them.

Rawlins took off his frock coat and draped it over the hitching rail beside him. Then he stepped down to the street and moved toward the middle of it. He felt sober and clearheaded except for a faint ringing sound in his ears.

John Stone continued to stride toward Rawlins. A boy had run into his office a few minutes ago and told him that Rawlins was going to have it out with Cooper, and then Stone heard two shots. Now he saw Rawlins in front of him, and guessed the worst.

"Morning, Rawlins," Stone said, stepping closer. "What happened?"

Akerson stood up on the sidewalk. "He shot Thad Cooper in cold blood!"

"It was a fair fight," Rawlins said. "He drawed on me."

"You egged him on," shouted a woman on the sidewalk, "and then you shot him."

"It's a lie," Rawlins said. "Thad Cooper drawed on me."

"Thad's gun isn't even out of its holster," Akerson told Stone.

"That's because I beat him to the draw," Rawlins replied.

Stone looked at Rawlins, and Rawlins looked like he'd been through hell. He'd heard that Rawlins had spent the night drinking at the Paradise and had broken up with Rosie.

"I'm afraid I'll have to ask you for your gun, Rawlins."

Rawlins sneered at him. "You must be crazy."

"You know the law better than I do." Stone took a step forward and held out his palm. "Hand it over."

Rawlins took a step backward. "Come and git it."

"Don't make this worse than it is, Rawlins."

"You want my gun, you come and git it."

Stone looked Rawlins in the eye and continued to move toward him, his left hand outstretched to receive the gun, and Rawlins stepped backward.

"Hand it over," Stone said.

"Don't crowd me, Stone."

"Give me that gun."

Rawlins stopped and planted his two feet squarely in the middle of the street. "Take another step and I'll kill you."

Stone saw the determined gleam in Rawlins's eyes and came to a halt six feet in front of him. Both men stared at each other.

"The first time I ever laid eyes on you," Rawlins said, "I knew it'd come to this."

"It doesn't have to," Stone replied. "Just hand over your gun, and let the judge decide. If you're innocent as you say, you'll go free."

"I don't trust the judge or anybody else around here," Rawlins said. "You'd all love to see me hang, don't think I don't know that."

"You'll get a fair trial."

Rawlins laughed. "Ain't no such thing. People around here don't know what fair is, and neither do you."

Stone held out his left hand again. "Give me that gun."

"I won't."

"I'll have to take it from you."

"Come on."

Stone hesitated a moment. He knew if he reached for Rawlins's gun, Rawlins would fight it out.

"You know what I've got to do, Buck. You were a lawman yourself."

"Make yer play," Rawlins said.

"I don't want to fight with you, Rawlins. I'm asking for your gun."

Rawlins tensed, dangled his hand above his holster. "Git ready to meet yer maker, you son of a bitch."

Stone stepped forward, his left hand raised to accept Rawlins's gun, and Rawlins's hand snapped down to his holster. In a motion so quick it was a blur, Stone drew his Colt and fired at point-blank range. The bullet hit Rawlins in the chest, just as Rawlins's fingers were drawing his gun from its holster. Rawlins pulled the trigger, and his bullet fired into the ground a few feet from Stone.

Rawlins stood limply in the street, smoke trailing out of his gun, a ferocious pain in his lungs. He stared at Stone in front of him, and Stone's gun still was pointing at him. Rawlins's mind was fogging quickly. He was aware of Rosie screaming somewhere nearby.

The next thing Rawlins knew he was on his knees in the middle of the street, and Rosie was beside him, trying to hold him steady. Rawlins looked up at Stone, who towered above him, his gun still in his hand.

"Chancellorsville," Rawlins uttered, and he sagged into Rosie's arms, his eyes closing, the battle over at last.

9

BUCK RAWLINS'S BODY lay in a coffin in front of the altar of
the Petie Church of God. The Reverend Vernon Scobie stood
a few feet away at the lectern, the light of candles bathing his
face in an orange glow as he eulogized the late sheriff of the
town. It was evening in Petie, and the sun was setting on the
mountains to the west of town.

Before Reverend Scobie, crowded into the pews, were the
townspeople in their mourning garb, sitting silently, while
in the background the organ was played by Mabel Billings, the portly president of the Ladies Auxiliary of the
church.

"He was a man with many faults," Reverend Scobie continued, "but we shouldn't let his faults obscure his virtues. He
was a brave man, and in the old days, when it wasn't safe to
walk down the main street of our town, he made it safe by
virtue of his courage and his gun, let's not forget that. He was
a man other men could look up to and admire."

Mayor Randlett sat in the front row with Jennifer and the
members of the town council, accompanied by their families.
Stone sat in the back row close to the door, his hat on his lap,

looking at the coffin on the bier. Rosie sat next to him, sobbing into a handkerchief.

Stone could make out Sheriff Rawlins's waxy profile, still as a statue, lying in ruffled satin, wearing his old frock coat. The town council had voted to let him be buried with his old sheriff's badge pinned to his lapel.

Stone was depressed. It wasn't hard to kill people he didn't know, but he'd known Rawlins and respected him. Rawlins had guts, but he'd gone rotten somewhere along the line, maybe it was too much whiskey.

Stone remembered Rawlins's last word: *Chancellorsville*, and wondered where that had come from. Had Rawlins fought at Chancellorsville too? Stone asked Rosie if she knew about Rawlins being at Chancellorsville, but she'd told Stone that Rawlins never talked much about the war, and Stone could understand that. He didn't like to talk about it either, because there was no point to it. The war was over and there were too many bad memories.

"This is the second funeral held in this town in two days," the Reverend Scobie said, "and let's face it, the man here in this coffin, Sheriff Buck Rawlins, was responsible for the first funeral, but let's not forget the example of Jesus, who forgave sinners and offered them salvation. And in the same spirit, I think we should forgive Sheriff Rawlins his sins. We should let God judge him and ask God to have mercy on his soul, just as we implore God to forgive our sins and have mercy on us, for as Jesus said: ' *Let he who is without sin cast the first stone*.' "

Brad Culhane sat on his horse and looked down at the lights of Petie shining in the night. On both sides of him were his men, pistols in their hands, ready to attack.

They'd arrived in the hills outside Petie earlier in the day, eaten a meal, and decided to attack the town as soon as it got dark.

Now it was dark, and a half moon shone in the sky overhead. The outlaws gazed down at the streets and buildings of Petie, hatred, lust, and greed in their hearts. They wanted to plunder and destroy the town where Deke Casey and his men had been killed, and in the future people would think twice before they started something with the men who'd ridden with Bloody Bill Anderson during the war.

Culhane looked to his left and right, his thick lips creased in a smile, as his horse anxiously pawed the prairie grass beneath its hooves. "There it is, boys," he said. "We come a long way to be here. Are you all ready?"

The men didn't say anything. They just sat firmly in their saddles as their horses danced and fidgeted beneath them. Their pistols were loaded and in their hands, ready to fire. They were eager to get moving.

Culhane raised his pistol high in the air. "Follow me!" he hollered. "Charge!"

He jabbed his spurs into his horse's flanks, and the animal bounded down the hill. His men followed on both sides of him, the hooves of their horses thundering against the prairie, the windstream rushing against their faces.

Culhane crouched low in his saddle, rocking smoothly with the long strides of his horse. The town was only a few hundred yards away, and soon they'd be there, with plenty of blood for everybody. He thought of Deke Casey, his friend and comrade during the war. "This one's fer you, Deke old boy," he muttered as he headed toward the main street of Petie.

The congregation was standing, singing a hymn as Mabel Billings pumped the pedals of the organ. Stone knew the words but didn't sing with the others. Somehow he couldn't bring himself to do it. Buck Rawlins was dead in his coffin up there, and Stone had killed him.

Stone searched his soul and wondered if there was any way he could've avoided killing Rawlins. *Maybe I should've just turned around and walked away.* But Rawlins had just shot Thad Cooper, and Stone was the deputy. He couldn't let Rawlins get away with it. It'd all come down to a matter of duty, and Stone was an old soldier: he took his duties seriously.

He thought he heard a distant shot, and perked up his ears. Then he heard another and wondered what was going on. Members of the congregation looked at one another as they sang; they heard the shots too.

Stone was sitting on the aisle in the last pew. He got up and walked back to the door of the church, opening it up.

The church was at the end of Main Street, and in the dim light at the center of town, he saw a large number of riders galloping about, firing their pistols. Smoke rose from a few of the downtown buildings. As Stone watched the riders, they came together and headed toward the church. A few moments later bullets slammed into the walls of the church.

He closed the doors and dropped to one knee. "Get down, everyone!"

The organ stopped suddenly, and the singing continued hesitantly for a few notes, then everything was silent except for the sound of gunfire outside, and bullets striking the church.

A baby began to cry. Stone moved toward the nearest window and looked outside. The riders charged toward the church, firing their pistols, and it looked like war.

Stone pulled out his two pistols and broke the glass window. He drew back the hammers and took aim at the riders galloping toward the church. Three of them carried lighted torches, and the others fired volleys at the church.

The riders continued their advance, and Stone took aim with both his pistols. The three with torches charged toward the windows, and Stone opened fire. He hit one of them, and one of the others threw his torch.

"That's for Deke Casey!" the rider yelled.

Stone dodged to the side, and the torch came crashing through the window, landing in the pews among the worshipers. Women shrieked, and everyone ran away. Bullets whizzed over their heads as the flames licked up the pews.

"Smother that fire!" Stone hollered. "You men—take your positions at the windows and start shooting!"

They all stared at him as if he were crazy. Another torch came crashing through a different window, sending glass and flames flying through the air. Women shrieked and children tugged their mothers' skirts.

Mayor Randlett broke through the crowd, his eyes glazed with horror. "What's going on out there?" he shouted.

"I don't know," Stone replied, "but we've got to fight back."

"Fight back? I'm not armed!"

"You'd better get armed."

Mayor Randlett stepped backward, his mouth hanging open. A bullet whizzed over his head and he dropped to his stomach on the floor.

Stone returned to the window and looked outside. The outlaws had turned around and were riding back through town, heading the other way, shooting at cowboys, drifters, and layabouts running for their lives in the downtown area.

In the church, groups of worshipers stamped out the flames and smothered the torches with their coats. Some of the men had drawn their pistols and were gathering around Stone.

"How many of you are armed?" Stone asked.

About half the men in the church, numbering approximately twenty-five, raised their hands.

"The town is evidently under attack by a band of outlaws who have something to do with Deke Casey," he told them. "We'll have to get weapons for those of us who don't have them, and the only weapons I know about are in my office. We'll go there through the back alley, with the women and children in the center, and the armed men on the outside. If they come at us while we're in the open, take cover and make every bullet count. Let's go."

Mayor Randlett raised his hand. "Just a moment," he said. "I'm not sure we want to get into a shooting war with those men out there."

"What other choice have you got?"

"Maybe we can wait until they go away."

"They'll go away all right, after they've finished killing whoever they want to kill, and doing whatever they feel like doing. There may not be anything left here when they leave. Is that what you want?"

Mayor Randlett looked confused. "Well . . . no."

Stone faced the members of the congregation standing in front of him. "You people'll have to make a choice, and you have to make it right now. Are you going to fight for your town, or aren't you? Those outlaws are shooting to kill. They'll do anything you let them do, and that includes killing you, burning down your town, and stealing everything you own. Are you going to let them do that, or are you going to fight?"

There was silence in the smoky church for a few seconds, as gunshots sounded in the distance. Then Phineas Mathers, owner of the Double M Ranch, spoke: "I say we fight!"

"So do I!" said Martin Caldwell, owner of Caldwell's General Store.

"Me too!" added Dr. Bill McGrath.

"How do the rest of you feel?" Stone asked.

Most of the men nodded or said in low, grim tones that they'd fight. Stone could see that they were frightened, but he'd led frightened men before. The only thing to do was take charge and set the proper example.

"Let's move out!" he said.

He marched toward the rear of the church, passing the coffin where Sheriff Rawlins lay in state, and the crowd of townspeople followed him. Opening the back door, he looked outside. The alleyway was clear. He stepped out, a pistol in each hand, and headed down the alley toward his office.

The townspeople shuffled behind him, women and children in the center, and the armed men were on the outside, ready to repulse an attack. They passed the privies and outbuildings scattered behind the main buildings of the town, and heard gunfire a short distance away.

Stone was in front, holding both his pistols in his hands. He could smell smoke and knew part of the town was on fire. Somehow they had to get to his office before the outlaws spotted them.

Then suddenly the gunfire stopped and everything became silent. Mayor Randlett was walking beside Stone, and he said, "I wonder what's happening now?"

"I don't know."

"Maybe they're leaving town."

"I wouldn't bet on that if I were you."

Brad Culhane raised his hand in the air, and his outlaw gang gathered around him in the darkness, smiles on their faces, smoke trailing from the barrels of their guns. Except for them, the main street of Petie was deserted. Several bodies lay dead or wounded on the sidewalk, and two buildings were smoldering. In front of them was the Petie Savings Bank.

Culhane was pleased with the way the attack had gone. There'd been no resistance and it appeared that the town was theirs.

"Let's git that money!" Culhane hollered.

The outlaws dismounted and tethered their horses to the hitching rail in front of the bank. Pulling out their pistols, they walked to the front door. Culhane twisted the knob, but the door was locked. He and his men aimed their pistols at the lock and opened fire. The door splintered and blew apart, bits of wood flying in all directions.

"That's enough!" Culhane said.

The door was shattered and the lock mangled badly. Culhane kicked the door and it opened wide. He stepped into the bank cautiously, holding his pistol aimed straight ahead, but no one was inside. His men followed him, walking behind the tellers' cage, opening drawers, dumping papers and records onto the floor, looking for money.

A door was at the rear of the tellers' cage, and Jubal Davidge shot the lock off it. He pushed the door open, leading a group of outlaws to the offices in back. They kicked chairs out of their way, tipped over desks, tore pictures off the walls, and threw the pictures into the hall.

"I found the safe!" yelled Clint Fulton.

Culhane and all the other outlaws stopped what they were doing and headed toward the office where Fulton was. It was the largest office in the bank and had a huge wooden desk in its middle, with the big black safe in the corner.

"Who's got the dynamite?" Culhane yelled.

Sand Kelly stepped forward, carrying the saddlebag full of dynamite. The other outlaws left the office as Kelly and Culhane placed bundles of dynamite sticks all around the safe.

"Light the fuses," Culhane said.

Kelly lit the fuses, and then he and Culhane joined the other outlaws in the hallway. They pressed their fingers into their ears and squinched their eyes.

The dynamite exploded with a terrible boom, smoke and debris filling the hallway. The outlaws waited a few moments, then rushed into the room.

The door of the safe was blown off and coins were scattered all over the floor. The outlaws got down on their hands and knees, scooping up the coins and dropping them into gunny sacks while Culhane reached into the safe and pulled out intact bags of money.

"Not a bad haul," he said with satisfaction.

The men cleaned every coin off the floor and took all the bags out of the safe. Then they checked the other offices to see if any more money was lying about, but there was none. Evidently all the money had been locked in the safe.

"Let's get out of here," Culhane said.

He walked toward the front door of the bank, and his men followed, carrying heavy sacks filled with money. They came to the sidewalk, and looked up and down the street. Culhane spotted the lights of the Paradise Saloon.

"Let's have a drink," he said.

"Don't you think we should git out of here?" Jubal Davidge replied.

"I'm thirsty," Culhane told him, "and besides, we got nothin' to worry about. The people in this town ain't got no fight in them. They're runnin' for the hills right now. We can do whatever we want here."

Culhane walked across the street toward the doors of the Paradise Saloon and threw them open. It was deserted inside, playing cards scattered across tables by gamblers who'd fled out the back door. Bottles and glasses of whiskey were everywhere. Culhane lifted a bottle off a table and raised it to his lips. It was his first drink of whiskey since they'd finished the bottles they'd stolen in Centerville, and it was delicious.

His men crowded into the saloon, grabbing bottles off tables or going behind the bar and opening fresh bottles.

Jubal Davidge sat down at the table with Brad Culhane. "I want me a woman," he said.

"What's yer hurry?" Culhane asked, sprawled out on a chair, his hat pushed to the back of his head.

"Ain't had a woman for a long time."

"We got all night. Enjoy yer whiskey, and after that we can find us some women. Bet there was lots of them in that church we was at."

Davidge drank some whiskey, his throat gurgling noisily. Culhane looked around at his other men, who'd taken over the saloon. One of them, Pinky Daniels, was playing "Dixie" on the piano, and a few of the others sang along with him.

"Wonder where the sheriff is?" Davidge asked.

Culhane snorted. "Prob'ly about ten miles out of town by

now, headin' for the hills with the rest of the damned cowards
who live around here."

Stone approached the back door of his office and pulled his
key ring out of his pocket. Behind him were the townspeople,
augmented by other men and women who'd been hiding in
the vicinity. Stone unlocked the door and passed through the
jail area, entering the main office. He opened the gun racks
and took down the rifles, passing them to the men filling
up the office. Then he unlocked the cupboards that held the
ammunition.

He heard footsteps on the sidewalk outside and spun around,
aiming his two pistols in that direction. A figure stopped in
front of the door and knocked softly. Stone advanced toward
the door and opened it. Toby Muldoon stood there, carrying
his new guitar.

"They robbed the bank," Muldoon said, "and now they's in
the Paradise Saloon. I was at the back door listenin' to 'em,
and I heard 'em say they was gonna start lookin' for the women
after they finished gittin' likkered up. They's a mean-lookin'
bunch if I ever saw one."

The women turned to one another and went pale. Some
of them hugged their husbands, hoping to find comfort and
strength, but their husbands were looking at John Stone,
waiting for him to tell them what to do.

Stone took the last rifle down from the rack and loaded it
up. Jennifer Randlett stood in the corner and watched him in
the darkness. He seemed to know exactly what he was doing,
and was calm and deliberate, unlike the rest of them.

Stone jacked a round into the chamber of the rifle and
looked up. "We should hit them right away, while they're
in the saloon. One bunch of us'll cover the back door,
and another bunch'll go in the front. We'll have to leave
some armed men here, to protect the women and children."
Walking across the room, Stone opened the foot locker filled
with the dynamite taken from Deke Casey's saddlebags. "We'll
bombard them with dynamite first," he continued. "That ought
to soften them up. Then we'll attack. Are there any questions?"

A hand arose in the darkness. "I own that saloon," a man

said. "Sounds to me like there won't be much left of it when you're finished."

"That's right," Stone said, "it'll probably sustain a considerable amount of damage, but there's no easy way out of this mess. Any other questions?"

Nobody said anything. Stone divided the men into three groups. The first group, led by Andy Thomaston, owner of the Diamond Restaurant, would guard the women and children left behind in the sheriff's office.

The second group, commanded by Phineas Mathers of the Double M Ranch, would watch the rear of the saloon, to stop any outlaws who might try to retreat.

The third group, under Stone, would assault the saloon from the front.

"Pick your shots and make them count," Stone said to them. "Remember that you're fighting for your town, your families, and everything that you've worked for all your lives." He looked at them and smiled. "Good luck to all of you. Move out."

Phineas Mathers led his group out the rear of the office and into the alley outside, heading toward the back of the Paradise Saloon. Stone opened the front door and looked both ways. The street was deserted except for a few bodies lying around. He motioned with his hand and ran across the street to the alley on the other side, and the town's male citizens followed him. They were young and old, tall and short, armed with rifles or pistols, some wearing suits, others dressed in range clothing. They disappeared into the alley and emerged at the rear of the building across the street, where Stone had shot Mike Chopak nearly a month ago.

Stone moved forward through the yards behind the row of buildings that faced the street, and the townspeople came behind him, the wan moonlight shining on the barrels of their guns. Stone held his rifle in both his hands and carried sticks of dynamite stuffed into his shirt. Several other men carried dynamite also. Mayor Randlett, slouching along behind Stone, was so afraid his teeth were chattering.

Finally they came to the buildings opposite the Paradise Saloon. Stone silently split the men into three groups and sent them through three alleys toward the street.

The men streamed through the alleys and arrived at the edge of the sidewalk. Before them were dead bodies lying in the street in front of the Paradise Saloon. Light blazed out the windows of the saloon, and laughter rang inside. Stone pulled a stick of dynamite out of his shirt. He wanted to wait a few minutes, to give Phineas Mathers and his men time to get into position. Taking a deep breath, he looked at the swinging doors of the Paradise. His men were ready, waiting for his signal. It was like the war and brought back memories of other attacks on other nights. He wondered if he'd be alive when this one was over.

Inside the saloon, Brad Culhane and his men were continuing their drunken celebration, bags of stolen money all around them. As far as they knew, they'd captured the town and chased the inhabitants away.

"Let's git started," said Jubal Davidge, sitting at a table with Brad Culhane. "I want to git me a woman."

"Wait'll I finish my whiskey," Culhane replied. "We just got here, for chrissakes."

"We been here too long. I'm gittin' nervous. It's too quiet."

"Davidge, if somebody gave you a pot of gold, you'd think there was somethin' wrong. You're never satisfied with what you got. Have another drink and you'll be all right."

"I don't want another drink. I want a woman."

"You'll git all you want—don't worry about it. Just lemme finish this bottle. Then we'll git started."

"Somethin's wrong," Davidge said, looking suspiciously from side to side. "Seems to me like these folks should've put up more of a fight."

"You got a lot to learn about folks, Davidge. The fact is that most of 'em are cowards who run at the sound of the first shot. So relax. I'm gittin' tired of yer bellyachin'."

Davidge scowled as he lit a cigarette. *I don't like this*, he thought. *We're wastin' too much time*.

Stone decided that Phineas Mathers and his men should be in their positions behind the Paradise Saloon. He raised his hand and pointed across the street, then moved out of the shadows.

The men carrying dynamite followed him silently across the street, passing dead bodies lying in the muck. Stone and the citizens of the town stepped onto the sidewalk, advancing on their tiptoes toward the doors. Stone stood next to the window and peered inside the saloon.

He saw the outlaws sitting around, drinking whiskey out of bottles, having a good time, and some were counting money, their eyes glittering with greed. Stone motioned for the citizens to prepare their dynamite, and they pulled the sticks out of their shirts, striking matches against the bottoms of their boots and lighting the fuses.

Stone edged toward the door and lit the fuse connected to his dynamite and, when it was fizzing, nodded to the others. Together they heaved their dynamite over the top of the swinging doors.

"Down!" Stone shouted.

He and the men with him dropped to the sidewalk, hearing shouts of panic inside the saloon. Two seconds later the dynamite exploded, and the ground shuddered beneath Stone's stomach. Orange light erupted through the window and doorway, followed by clouds of smoke and horrified screams.

"Now!"

Stone jumped to his feet and charged through the doors of the saloon, into the swirling smoke and broken furniture. He saw figures moving in the darkness and fired his rifle from the waist, working the lever as quickly as he could.

His men poured through the doorway behind him, shooting at anything that moved. Most of the outlaws had been killed or wounded in the initial explosions, and the rest were dazed and disoriented. The men of Petie mowed them down, showing no mercy, the sound of gunshots and screams reverberating off the shattered walls.

"Hold your fire!" Stone shouted.

The men eased their fingers off their triggers as the smoke cleared. A scene of total devastation faced them. Blood and gore were everywhere, furniture and men had been blown to bits, coins were scattered all over the floor, and the painting on the wall was split in two. A few wounded outlaws who miraculously hadn't been killed feebly begged for help.

"My saloon is ruined," said a voice in darkness.

"We'll help you rebuild," replied Mayor Randlett. "Don't worry about that, but first we've got to put out the fires in this town."

Mayor Randlett gave orders for the fire brigades, and Stone moved back into a corner, sitting on a chair, reaching for his bag of tobacco. He heard the whimpers of the few wounded outlaws who'd miraculously survived, and saw the townspeople run outside to fight the fires. Dr. McGrath arrived with his black bag and began to treat the wounded outlaws.

Dr. McGrath noticed Stone in the corner. "Are you all right, Sheriff?" he asked, kneeling beside the body of Jubal Davidge, whose shirt was soaked with blood.

"I'm not your sheriff anymore," Stone replied. "It's time I was moving on."

"You can't leave us now," Dr. McGrath argued. "It wouldn't be right. Didn't you say you'd stay until we found somebody else to maintain law and order around here?"

"You have found somebody else," Stone said. "Yourselves."

10

THE NEXT EVENING, Stone was seated with Mayor and Jennifer Randlett in the dining room of their mansion on the hill. The main course was baked ham and yams with collard greens, and the men drank fine bourbon whiskey.

The room was lit by candles, and the light flickered on Mayor Randlett's corpulent face. "John," he said, "what can we do to make you stay?"

"Nothing," Stone replied, wearing a shirt and jeans freshly scrubbed and ironed by the girls at Miss Elsie's place. "It's time for me to move on."

"We wish you wouldn't do that, John. You've done a lot for this town and we don't want to see you leave, but I can understand why you wouldn't want to be sheriff anymore. It's a dangerous job and doesn't have much of a future. But there are other things you could do here in Petie. Do you think you might be interested in something else?"

"Such as?"

"Name it and it's yours," Mayor Randlett said. "Let's not beat around the bush. I own this town and I can do anything I want. I believe you said once that you wanted to become a rancher. We can set you up on your own ranch, lend you whatever money you need at reasonable terms. This town needs a man like you, and you could have a brilliant future here. A rolling stone gathers no moss, you know. You're young and strong now, but where will you be thirty or forty years down the road? Think about all the old worn-out cowboys like Toby Muldoon that you see in every town on the frontier. They were young and healthy like you once, but they never settled down. Do you want to end up like one of them?"

Stone thought of Muldoon, an alcoholic forced to beg strangers for money. "No, I wouldn't, but I'm looking for somebody."

Mayor Randlett leaned forward. "What if you're just chasing a dream, a chimera? What if you spend your whole life searching for somebody, and never find her? What then?"

"I try not to think of that, Mayor. I try to think that I'll find her."

"You have no guarantee that you'll find her, and where is she anyway? Why didn't she leave word for you? That's what she would've done if she cared about you and wanted you to follow her. Have you ever stopped to think about that?"

Stone looked up from his plate of food. "I can see that you're a fine lawyer, because your arguments are very persuasive, but you don't understand. I'm in love with the woman and I have to find her."

"Love?" asked Mayor Randlett. "What's love? Poets and philosophers have tried to figure it out since the dawn of time, and they've never done it yet, to my knowledge. Let me tell you something, John: A bird in the hand is worth two in the bush. It's an old saying but it's true. On one hand I'm offering you a ranch and a future, and on the other hand what do you have? A dream, a fantasy, maybe even a form of madness? Take a step back from the situation and think it over. You don't have to give your answer now. But give it some thought. Don't dismiss it so quickly. It's a big decision. An opportunity like this comes along once in a lifetime."

That night Stone lay in bed in the attic above Miss Elsie's place and thought about what Mayor Randlett had said. His window was open and the drapes were pulled back so he could see stars blazing in the sky above the wide prairie.

He realized that Mayor Randlett was offering him a fabulous opportunity. It'd be wonderful to own his own ranch, raise his own cattle, maybe even breed horses on the side. The financial part wouldn't be a problem, because as Mayor Randlett said, he owned the bank and nearly everything else in the area. Mayor Randlett could make it happen.

Mayor Randlett liked him and wanted him to stay, and Petie was as good a place as any to settle down. It was true: a rolling stone gathered no moss. He was just a poor drifter with a few dollars in his pocket, and life could be cruel when a man got old. He thought of Toby Muldoon and all the other old cowboys who hung around the saloons of frontier towns, and shuddered when he realized he could wind up like that: penniless, weak, raggedy and toothless, begging for coins.

He recalled Jennifer Randlett sitting to his side at the table. She hadn't said much during the dinner meal, but she'd been utterly beautiful, wearing a gown that showed her smooth bare shoulders. Stone knew that she was part of the deal, and a man couldn't ask for a better wife.

He saw a wonderful future unfolding ahead of him. No longer would he have to sleep on the prairie with his saddle for a pillow and nothing except an old moth-eaten blanket to protect him from the wind and rain. No longer would he be the stranger riding into towns, with the local people eyeing him suspiciously, and there was always a crazy drunken cowboy around who wanted to fight.

Stone closed his eyes. All he wanted was an ordinary life with Marie, but where was she? Maybe Mayor Randlett was right. Maybe he was chasing a fantasy that could become a nightmare when he became old.

He felt agitated and couldn't sleep. Rolling out of bed, he lit the lamp on the night-table, then rolled a cigarette. He reached to the bedpost, took down his shirt, and pulled the photograph of Marie out of the shirt pocket.

He sat on the edge of the bed and puffed the cigarette as he looked at the picture of Marie. They'd been like two components of the same being, but where was she now? Mayor Randlett's argument had made sense. If Marie still loved him or wanted to see again, wouldn't she have waited for him back in South Carolina after the war? Or if she had to go away, why didn't she leave a message?

It was incredible that she'd disappear without a word, but that was what happened. Maybe she'd fallen in love with someone else and didn't know how to break it to Stone. The war had changed a lot of people, including himself, and maybe it had changed Marie too. Maybe she thought that their love had just been a youthful fancy, not the kind of thing she could build her life on. Maybe she'd fallen out of love with him and didn't care about him at all anymore.

"Why didn't you write to me?" he asked the picture. "Why did you just disappear without saying anything?"

Stone had thought their love would last forever, even enduring beyond the grave, but now he wasn't so sure. He was searching for her across the length and breadth of the frontier, and maybe she'd completely forgotten about him.

Once again he found himself questioning the validity of his search. On the one hand he had Jennifer Randlett, with her flaming red hair and green eyes, plus a ranch all his own, and on the other hand he had dusty trails and broken-down cattle towns, lonely days and lonelier nights.

Stone looked down at the photograph and didn't know what to do. Mayor Randlett had offered him a chance for happiness, and he couldn't turn it down so easily, but how could he forget the love that had left its own special brand on his heart?

A wave of confusion passed over him. It was as though Marie held him by one arm, and Jennifer by the other, and both of them were pulling him apart.

He was tempted by Mayor Randlett's offer, but he wanted Marie. He felt that he'd never be able to rest until he solved the mystery of her disappearance.

He puffed his cigarette and realized that was the crux of his dilemma. He could marry Jennifer and wind up owning the finest ranch in the territory, but he'd never be happy. He'd spend the rest of his life wondering what had happened to Marie, worrying that she needed him, and it would undermine his happiness, eating into his soul.

He'd pretend he was happy with Jennifer, but knew he'd never forget Marie. He'd love the children he'd have with

Jennifer, but he'd always wonder if he might've loved the children he had with Marie more.

He and Marie had grown up together. He'd loved her even when he was a boy, and he'd love her all his life. He held the picture of Marie up to the light, and the expression in her eyes cut deeply into him. It was as if she were pleading with him not to abandon her, because she needed him.

She was his first and only love, and he'd never had anything to do with any other woman. He knew that no matter where she was and what she was doing, she wouldn't be able to forget him, just as he hadn't been able to forget her. He'd always thought God had brought them together, and nothing could ever break them apart.

He might wind up as a lonely old derelict someday, just like Toby Muldoon, but at least he'd know that he tried to fulfill his destiny. He might never find Marie, but he had to try. Hardship, danger, and lonely nights lay ahead of him, but he saw no choice. He'd never forget her, no matter how many ranches he owned and how many Jennifers he married. He might be chasing a dream, but it was the best dream he had.

He clenched his jaw and balled up his fists. Then he arose and put on his clothes. He strapped on his gunbelts and picked up his rifle and saddlebags.

Descending the stairs to the kitchen, he tossed a few cans of beans and some biscuits into the saddlebags. He left by the rear entrance and walked toward the center of town. At Mayor Randlett's office, he unpinned his tin badge and dropped it into the mailbox, along with the keys to the sheriff's office.

He headed toward the stable, keeping in the shadows where no one could see him. He didn't want to say good-bye to anybody or make explanations or excuses. He didn't think anybody could understand his quest. He wasn't sure he understood it himself.

He passed the Paradise Saloon, heard the laughter and the piano. It'd be nice to go in for one last drink, but one last drink would lead to two, and before he knew it he'd be living on a ranch with Jennifer and a bunch of kids, hating himself for turning away from the one true love of his life.

"Goin' somewheres, Cap'n?"

Stone stopped in his tracks. Ahead of him, sitting on the

bench in front of Bob's Barbershop, was Toby Muldoon, his new guitar leaning beside him.

"I'm on my way out of town," Stone told him.

"Why's that, Cap'n?"

"Just a drifter, I guess."

"Buy me a drink?"

Stone flipped Muldoon a few coins. Although it was dark, the old bum snatched them out of the air.

"Happy trails to you, Cap'n," Muldoon said. "If you ever find that gal you're lookin' fer, give her a kiss fer me."

Stone walked past him, heading for the stable. He found Mortimer in his stall, and the big black horse looked at him curiously.

"We're moving on," Stone told him.

Stone saddled the horse and put on the bridle. Then he walked to the office, woke up the man, and paid him for taking care of Mortimer.

"Where you headed?" the man asked sleepily.

Stone shrugged, because he didn't even know himself. He returned to the stall where Mortimer was, and climbed into the saddle.

He rode out of the stable and down the main street of Petie, the sound of the horse's hooves echoing off storefronts closed for the night. It was deserted in that part of town, and ahead was the open range.

Stone wasn't sure he was doing the right thing. He couldn't say for sure what the right thing was anymore, but he didn't dare look back at the town that had given him the opportunity to lead a new life.

He didn't want a new life. He wasn't finished yet with the one he had.

He rode onto the prairie and disappeared into the night.

A special offer for people who enjoy reading the best Westerns published today. If you enjoyed this book, subscribe now and get . . .

TWO FREE

A $5.90 VALUE—NO OBLIGATION

If you enjoyed this book and would like to read more of the very best Westerns being published today, you'll want to subscribe to True Value's Western Home Subscription Service. If you enjoyed the book you just read and want more of the most exciting, adventurous, action packed Westerns, subscribe now.

Each month the editors of True Value will select the 6 very best Westerns from America's leading publishers for special readers like you. You'll be able to preview these new titles as soon as they are published, FREE for ten days with no obligation.

TWO FREE BOOKS

When you subscribe, we'll send you your first month's shipment of the newest and best 6 Westerns for you to preview. With your first shipment, two of these books will be yours as our introductory gift to you absolutely FREE, regardless of what you decide to do. If you like them, as much as we think you will, keep all six books but pay for just 4 at the low subscriber rate of just $2.45 each. If you decide to return them, keep 2 of the titles as our gift. No obligation.

Special Subscriber Savings

When you become a True Value subscriber you'll save money several ways. First, all regular monthly selections will be billed at the low subscriber price of just $2.45 each. That's

WESTERNS!

at least a savings of $3.00 each month below the publishers price. Second, there is never any shipping, handling or other hidden charges—Free home delivery. What's more there is no minimum number of books you must buy, you may return any selection for full credit and you can cancel your subscription at any time. A TRUE VALUE!

Mail the coupon below

To start your subscription and receive 2 FREE WESTERNS, fill out the coupon below and mail it today. We'll send your first shipment which includes 2 FREE BOOKS as soon as we receive it.

Mail To:
True Value Home Subscription Services, Inc.   4631-B
P.O. Box 5235
120 Brighton Road
Clifton, New Jersey 07015-5235

YES! I want to start receiving the very best Westerns being published today. Send me my first shipment of 6 Westerns for me to preview FREE for 10 days. If I decide to keep them, I'll pay for just 4 of the books at the low subscriber price of $2.45 each; a total of $9.80 (a $17.70 value). Then each month I'll receive the 6 newest and best Westerns to preview Free for 10 days. If I'm not satisfied I may return them within 10 days and owe nothing. Otherwise I'll be billed at the special low subscriber rate of $2.45 each; a total of $14.70 (at least a $17.70 value) and save $3.00 off the publishers price. There are never any shipping, handling or other hidden charges. I understand I am under no obligation to purchase any number of books and I can cancel my subscription at any time, no questions asked. In any case the 2 FREE books are mine to keep.

Name _____

Address _____ Apt. # _____

City _____ State _____ Zip _____

Telephone # _____

Signature _____
                        (if under 18 parent or guardian must sign)
              Terms and prices subject to change.
    Orders subject to acceptance by True Value Home Subscription Services, Inc.